THIS BOOK
BELONGS TO:

The Nursery Collection

Stories & Rhymes for the Very Young

This is a Parragon Publishing Book
This edition published in 2001

Parragon Publishing
Queen Street House, 4 Queen Street,
Bath, BA1 1HE, UK

Produced by The Templar Company Plc
Pippbrook Mill, London Road, Dorking,
Surrey, RH4 1JE, UK

Designed by Kilnwood Graphics

Printed and bound in China
ISBN 0 75254 105 6

The Nursery Collection

Stories & Rhymes for the Very Young

A collection of traditional rhymes, and original material written by
Caroline Repchuk, Claire Keen and Andrew Charman

Contents

Here We Go Round the Mulberry Bush

Here we go round the mulberry bush,
mulberry bush, mulberry bush,
Here we go round the mulberry bush,
on a cold and frosty morning.

This is the way we brush our hair,
brush our hair, brush our hair,
This is the way we brush our hair,
on a cold and frosty morning.

Repeat chorus

This is the way we clap our hands,
clap our hands, clap our hands,
This is the way we clap our hands,
on a cold and frosty morning.

Repeat chorus

This is the way we fall on the floor,
fall on the floor, fall on the floor,
This is the way we fall on the floor,
on a cold and frosty morning.

Repeat chorus

Oranges and Lemons

Oranges and lemons,

Say the bells of St Clements.

I owe you five farthings,

Say the bells of St Martins.

When will you pay me?

Say the bells of Old Bailey.

When I grow rich,

Say the bells of Shoreditch.

Rub-A-Dub-Dub

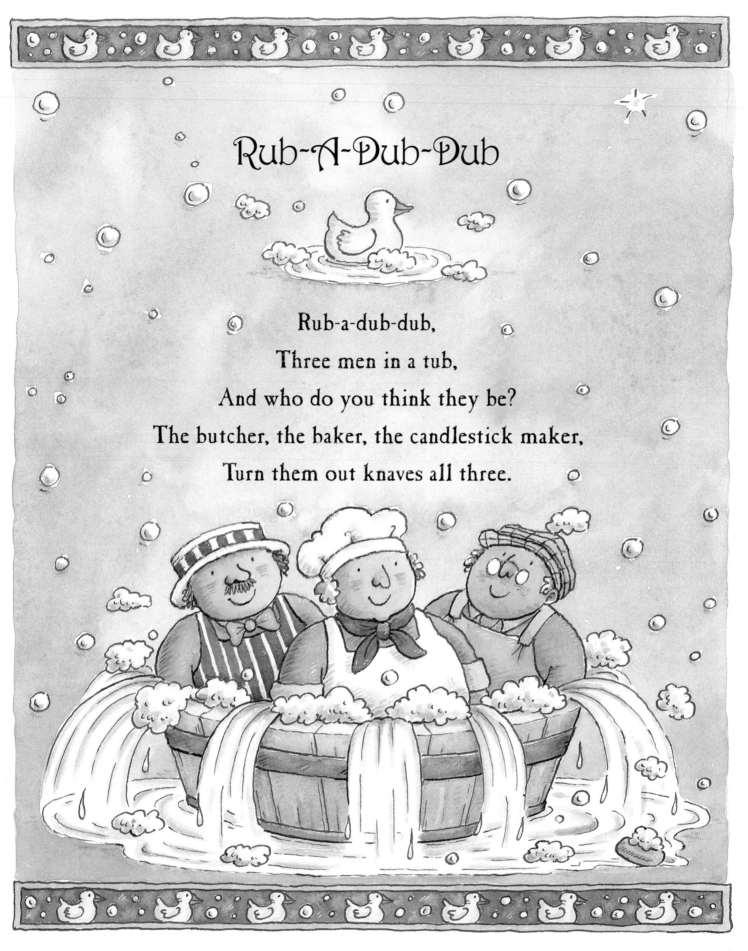

Rub-a-dub-dub,
Three men in a tub,
And who do you think they be?
The butcher, the baker, the candlestick maker,
Turn them out knaves all three.

Round and Round the Garden

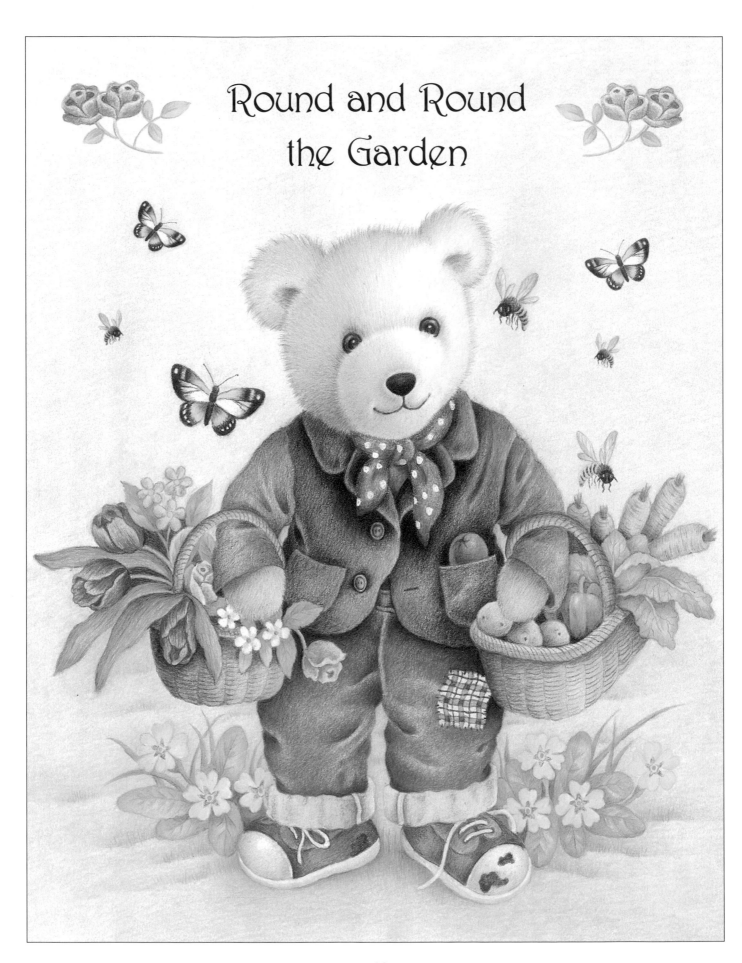

Round and round
the garden,
Like a teddy bear;

One step, two steps,
Tickle you under there!

Round and round
the haystack,
Went the little mouse.

One step, two steps,
In this little house.

Circle palm

Walk fingers up arm

Tickle!

ROUND AND ROUND

ONE STEP, TWO STEP

TICKLE!

Baa Baa Black Sheep

Baa, baa, black sheep,
Have you any wool?
Yes, sir, yes, sir,
Three bags full;
One for the master,
And one for the dame,
And one for the little boy
Who lives down the lane.

Hot Cross Buns!

Hot cross buns!

Hot cross buns!

One a-penny, two a-penny,

Hot cross buns!

If you have no daughters,

Give them to your sons,

One a-penny, two a-penny,

Hot cross buns!

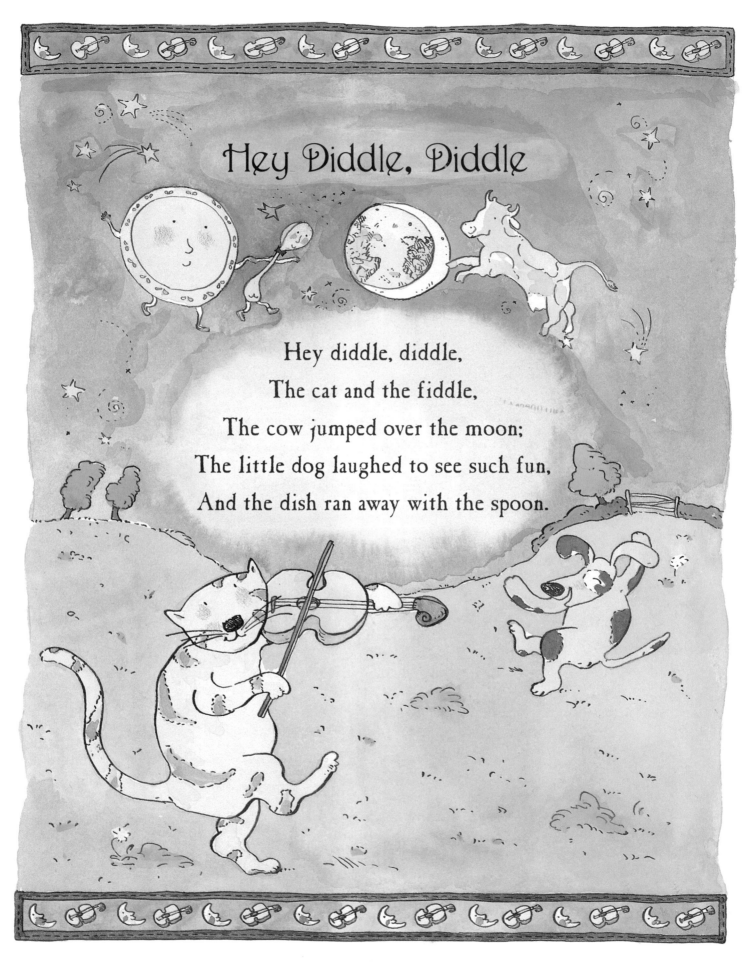

Hey Diddle, Diddle

Hey diddle, diddle,
The cat and the fiddle,
The cow jumped over the moon;
The little dog laughed to see such fun,
And the dish ran away with the spoon.

Little Bo Peep

Little Bo Peep has lost her sheep
And doesn't know where to find them;
Leave them alone, and they'll come home
Bringing their tails behind them.

CROCODILE SMILES

"Say cheese!" said the photographer.

"CHEESE!" grinned Snappy, the crocodile. Lights flashed, and cameras clicked as he gave his most winning smile.

"You're a natural!" cried the expedition leader. He was with a team of wildlife photographers. Snappy smiled at his reflection in the river.

"Ooh, you are a handsome chap!" he preened, gnashing his fine set of teeth together with glee.

Snappy was terribly proud of his sharp fangs, and fine good looks. He strutted up and down the river bank for all to see.

"I'm a star!" he said. "My face will be known throughout the world!"

"Thanks for letting us take your picture," said the expedition leader.

"No problem," said Snappy. "Anytime!"

"And as your reward, here's the truckload of chocolate you asked for," said the leader.

"How delicious!" said Snappy. "Most kind of you. Thank you so much."

When they had gone, Snappy lay sunning himself on the river bank, daydreaming of fame and fortune, and popping chocolate after chocolate into his big, open mouth.

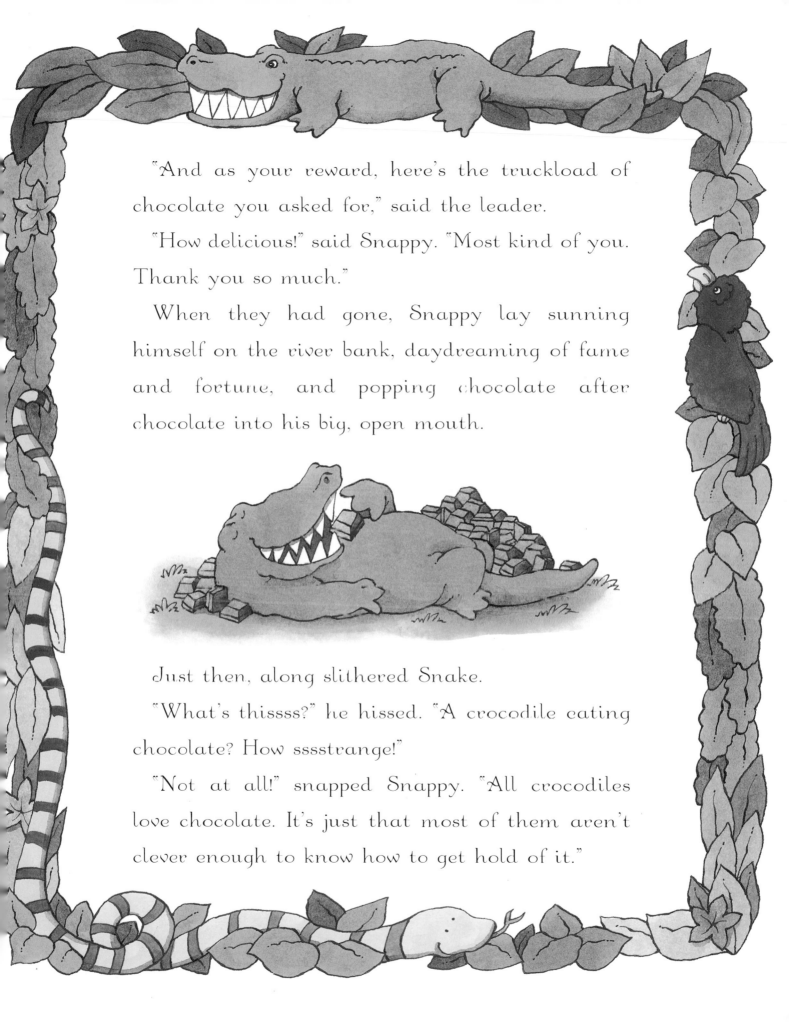

Just then, along slithered Snake.

"What's thissss?" he hissed. "A crocodile eating chocolate? How sssstrange!"

"Not at all!" snapped Snappy. "All crocodiles love chocolate. It's just that most of them aren't clever enough to know how to get hold of it."

"Well, if you're so sssmart, you ssshould know that too much chocolate will make your teeth fall out!" hissed Snake.

"What rot!" said Snappy, crossly. "For your information, I've got perfect teeth."

"Lucky you!" said Snake, and slithered off into the bushes.

So Snappy carried on munching happily, eating his way through the mound of chocolate. He had chocolate for breakfast, chocolate for lunch and chocolate for dinner.

"Ooh, yummy!" he grinned, licking his lips and smiling a big, chocolatey smile. "This is heaven."

"You won't be saying that when you are too fat to float in the river," said Parrot, who had been watching him from a tree.

"Nonsense!" scoffed Snappy. "I've got a very fine figure, I'll have you know!"

"If you say so," said Parrot, and flew off into the jungle.

Days and weeks passed, and Snappy happily carried on eating chocolate after chocolate, until at last it was all gone.

"Back to the river to catch my next meal, then," Snappy thought miserably. "Though I'd much rather have more chocolate!"

But when Snappy slid into the river, instead of bobbing gently at the surface, he sank straight to the bottom, and his stomach rested in the mud.

"Oh, dear, what's happened to the river?" Snappy wondered aloud to himself. "It's very hard to float in today."

"Even for someone with such a fine figure as you?" jeered Parrot, watching from the trees. Snappy didn't answer. He just sank further beneath the water so that only his two beady eyes could be seen, and gave Parrot a very hard stare.

The next morning when he awoke there was a terrible pain in his mouth. It felt like someone was twisting and tugging on his teeth. "Oww, my teeth hurt!" he cried.

"Sssurely not!" hissed Snake, dangling down from a tree. "After all, you have sssuch perfect teeth!" and he slunk away again, snickering.

Snappy knew what he had to do. He set off down the river to visit Mr Drill the dentist.

29

It seemed such a long hard walk, and by the time he got there he was puffing and panting.

"Open wide!" said Mr Drill, an anteater, peering down his long nose into Snappy's gaping mouth. "Oh, dear. This doesn't look good at all. What have you been eating, Snappy? Now show me where it hurts."

"Here," said Snappy pointing miserably into his mouth, and feeling rather ashamed, "and here, and here, and here..."

"Well, there's nothing for it," said Mr Drill, "they'll have to come out!" And so out they came!

Before long, another photography expedition arrived in the jungle.

"Say cheese!" said the expedition leader.

"CHEESE!" smiled Snappy, stepping out from behind a tree. But instead of a flash of cameras, Snappy met with howls of laughter, as the photographers fell about holding their sides.

"I thought you said Snappy was a handsome crocodile with perfect teeth!" they cried, looking at the leader. "He should be called Gappy, not Snappy!"

Poor Snappy slunk away into the bushes and cried. It was all his own fault for being so greedy and eating all that chocolate.

"There, there," said Mr Drill, patting his arm. "We'll soon fit you out with some fine new teeth."

And from then on, Snappy vowed he would never eat chocolate again!

If You're Happy and You Know It

If you're happy and you know it,
Clap your hands.
If you're happy and you know it,
Clap your hands.
If you're happy and you know it,
And you really want to show it,
If you're happy and you know it,
Clap your hands.

If you're happy and you know it,
Nod your head, etc.
If you're happy and you know it,
Stamp your feet, etc.

If you're happy and you know it,
Say "ha, ha!", etc.
If you're happy and you know it,
Do all four!

Georgie Porgie

Georgie Porgie, pudding and pie,
Kissed the girls and made them cry;
When the boys came out to play,
Georgie Porgie ran away.

Three Blind Mice

Three blind mice, three blind mice
See how they run, see how they run!
They all ran after the farmer's wife,
Who cut off their tails with a carving knife,
Did you ever see such a thing in your life,
As three blind mice?!

FIVE LITTLE DUCKLINGS

One, two, three, four, five,
Five little ducklings duck and dive,
Six, seven, eight, nine, ten,
Then swim home in a row again!

Why do they swim in rows?
The answer is nobody knows!
I wonder, as they swim past,
Who goes first and who goes last?

To the tune of 'Once I Caught A Fish Alive.'

CAT'S CHORUS

We meet every night
On the same garden wall,
And if you're in luck
You may hear our call:
With howl and a yowl, and a hullaballoo,
We're the cat's chorus, singing for you!

Fifi's soprano,
Butch sings the bass,
Kipper's a baritone,
Bert sets the pace.

Chorus

We sing lots of songs
Both new ones and old,
All huddled together
To keep out the cold.

Chorus

I Hear Thunder

(To the tune of Frère Jacques)

I hear thunder,
I hear thunder,
Oh! Don't you?
Oh! Don't you?

Pitter, patter raindrops,
Pitter, patter raindrops,
I'm wet through,
I'm wet through.

Pretend to listen

I HEAR THUNDER

Flutter hands like rain

PITTER, PATTER RAINDROPS

Wrap arms around body

I'M WET THROUGH

Hurry up the sunshine,
Hurry up the sunshine,
I'll soon dry,
I'll soon dry.

I see blue skies,
I see blue skies,
Way up high,
Way up high.

Point up to sky

WAY UP HIGH

Circle hands in front of chest

HURRY UP THE SUNSHINE

Pretend to shake hands dry

I'LL SOON DRY

BARNEY THE BOASTFUL BEAR

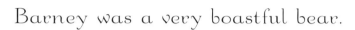

Barney was a very boastful bear.

"Look at my lovely soft fur!" he would say to the other toys. "See how it shines!"

Barney loved to talk about himself. "I'm the smartest toy in the playroom!" he would say. "It's a well-known fact."

He didn't know that the other toys all laughed about him behind his back.

"That bear thinks he's so smart," growled Scotty Dog. "But he isn't smart enough to know when everyone's fed up with him!"

"He'll learn his lesson one of these days," said Molly Monkey, and sure enough, that is just what happened...

One hot summer's day, the toys lazed in the warm playroom. "Wouldn't it be lovely if we could go for a walk outside," said Rag Doll.

"We could have a lovely picnic in the woods!" said Old Bear.

"Even better, we could go for a drive in the toy car first!" said Rabbit.

"But none of us is big or clever enough to drive the toy car," said Rag Doll, sadly.

"I am!" came a voice from the corner. It was Barney. He had been listening to them talking.

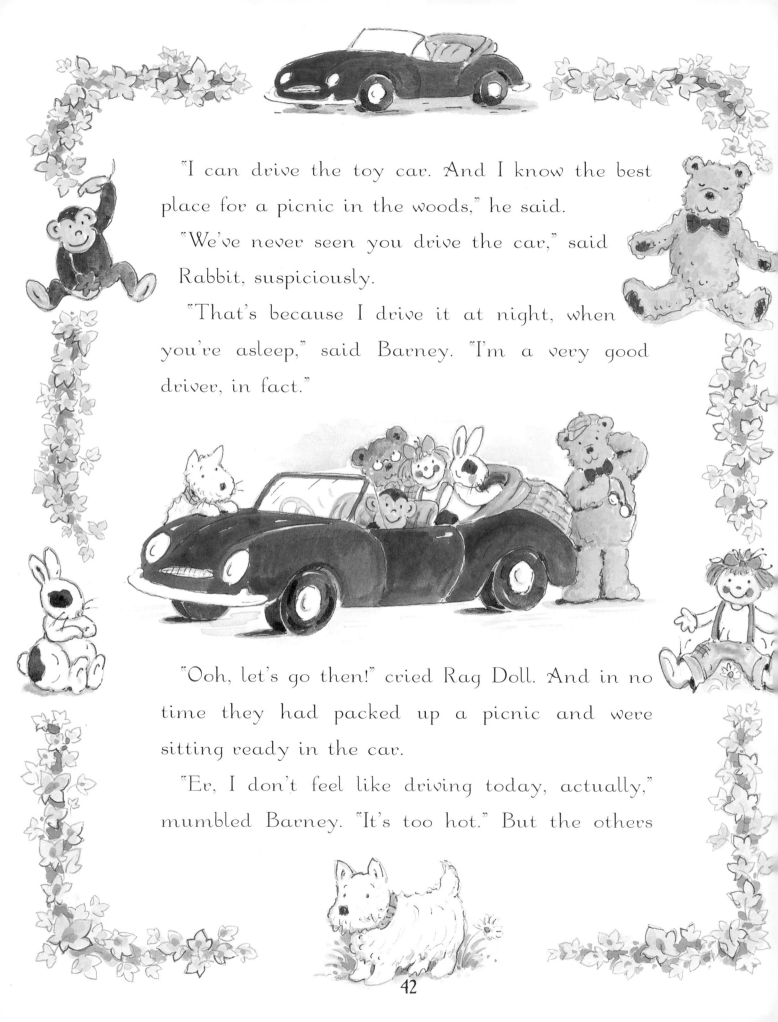

"I can drive the toy car. And I know the best place for a picnic in the woods," he said.

"We've never seen you drive the car," said Rabbit, suspiciously.

"That's because I drive it at night, when you're asleep," said Barney. "I'm a very good driver, in fact."

"Ooh, let's go then!" cried Rag Doll. And in no time they had packed up a picnic and were sitting ready in the car.

"Er, I don't feel like driving today, actually," mumbled Barney. "It's too hot." But the others were not interested in hearing excuses, so rather reluctantly Barney climbed into the driver's seat and started the engine. You see, the truth was, Barney had never really driven the car before, and he was scared. But he wanted to show off, so he pretended to know what he was doing.

Off they set down the garden path. "Toot, toot!" Barney beeped the horn as he turned the little car out into the country lane, and soon they were driving along, singing merrily.

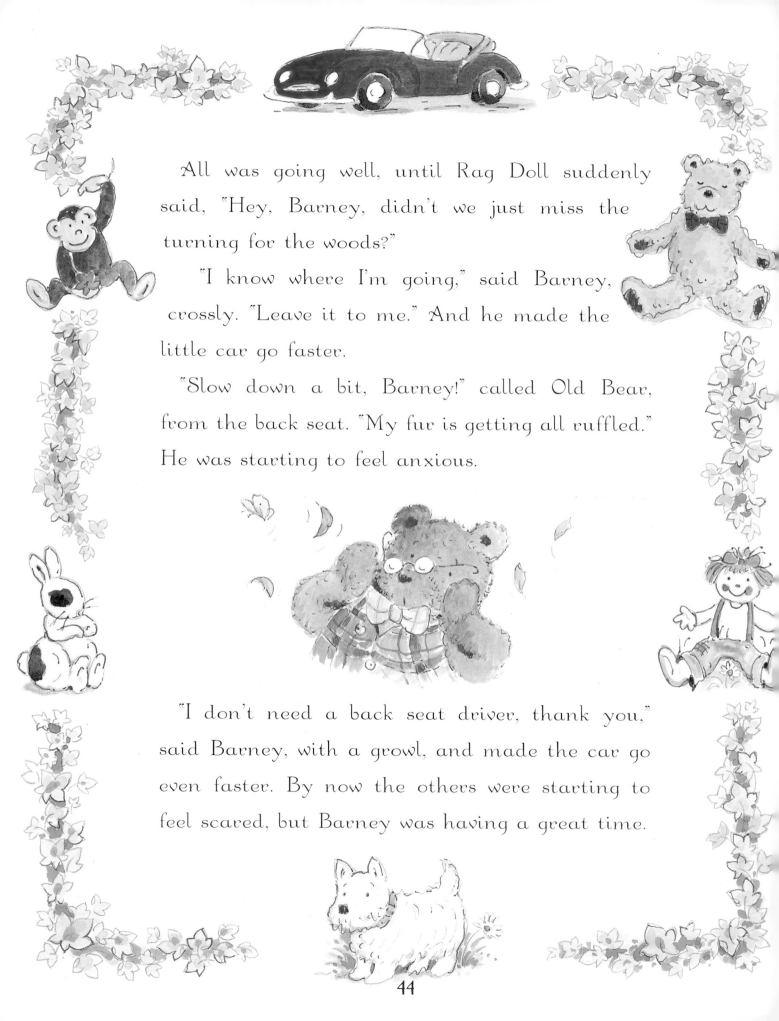

All was going well, until Rag Doll suddenly said, "Hey, Barney, didn't we just miss the turning for the woods?"

"I know where I'm going," said Barney, crossly. "Leave it to me." And he made the little car go faster.

"Slow down a bit, Barney!" called Old Bear, from the back seat. "My fur is getting all ruffled." He was starting to feel anxious.

"I don't need a back seat driver, thank you," said Barney, with a growl, and made the car go even faster. By now the others were starting to feel scared, but Barney was having a great time.

"Aren't I a wonderful driver!" he chuckled. "Look — no hands!" And he took his paws off the steering wheel. Just then they reached a sharp corner. The little car went spinning off the side of the road and crashed into a tree, tipping all the toys out into the ditch!

They were a bit dazed, but luckily no one was hurt. They were not pleased with Barney though. "You silly bear!" said Rabbit, crossly. "We could have all been badly hurt!"

"We'll have to walk home now," said Rag Doll, rubbing her head. "Where are we?"

Everyone looked at Barney.

"Don't ask me!" he said, quietly.

"But you said you knew the way!" said Old Bear, indignantly.

"I was only pretending," said Barney, his voice trembling. "I don't really know how to drive, and I don't know where we are!" And he started to cry.

The other toys were furious with Barney.

"You naughty boastful bear!" they scolded. "Now see what trouble your boasting has got us into!"

The lost toys walked through the dark woods all night long, clinging together in fright as shadows loomed around them.

They had never been out at night before. Then just before dawn, they spotted the little house where they lived, and crept back into the playroom.

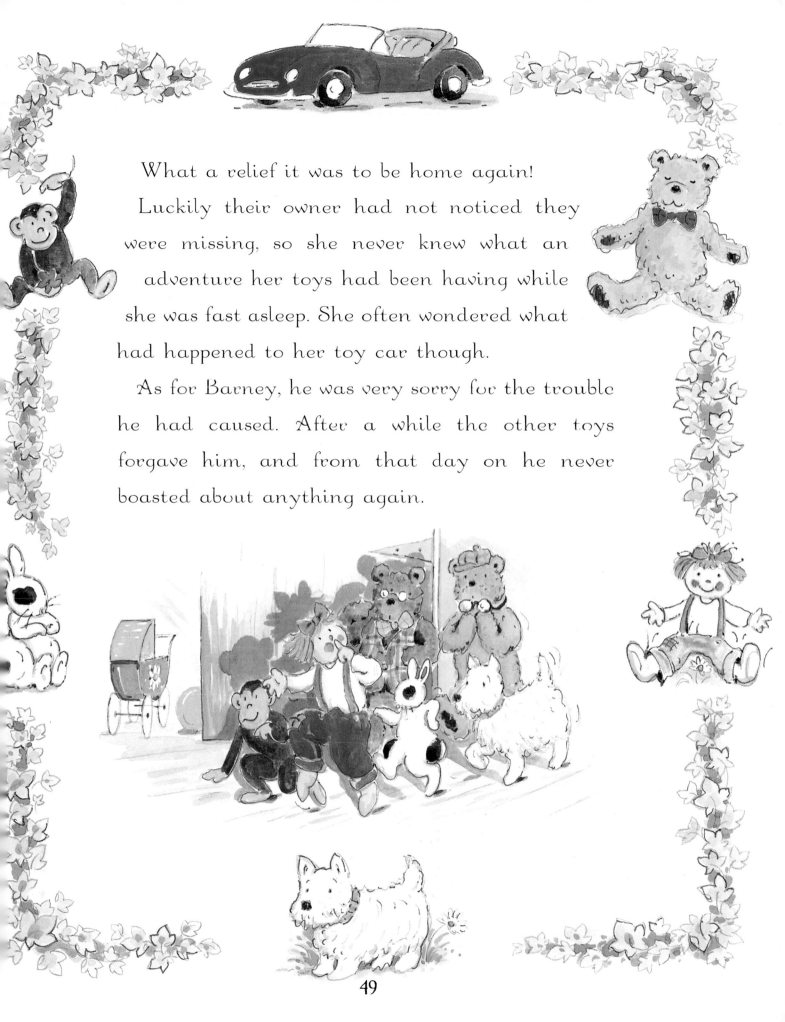

What a relief it was to be home again! Luckily their owner had not noticed they were missing, so she never knew what an adventure her toys had been having while she was fast asleep. She often wondered what had happened to her toy car though.

As for Barney, he was very sorry for the trouble he had caused. After a while the other toys forgave him, and from that day on he never boasted about anything again.

I Love Little Pussy

I love little pussy,
her coat is so warm,
And if I don't hurt her
she'll do me no harm.
So I'll not pull her tail,
nor drive her away,
But Pussy and I very
gently will play.

I Had a Little Nut Tree

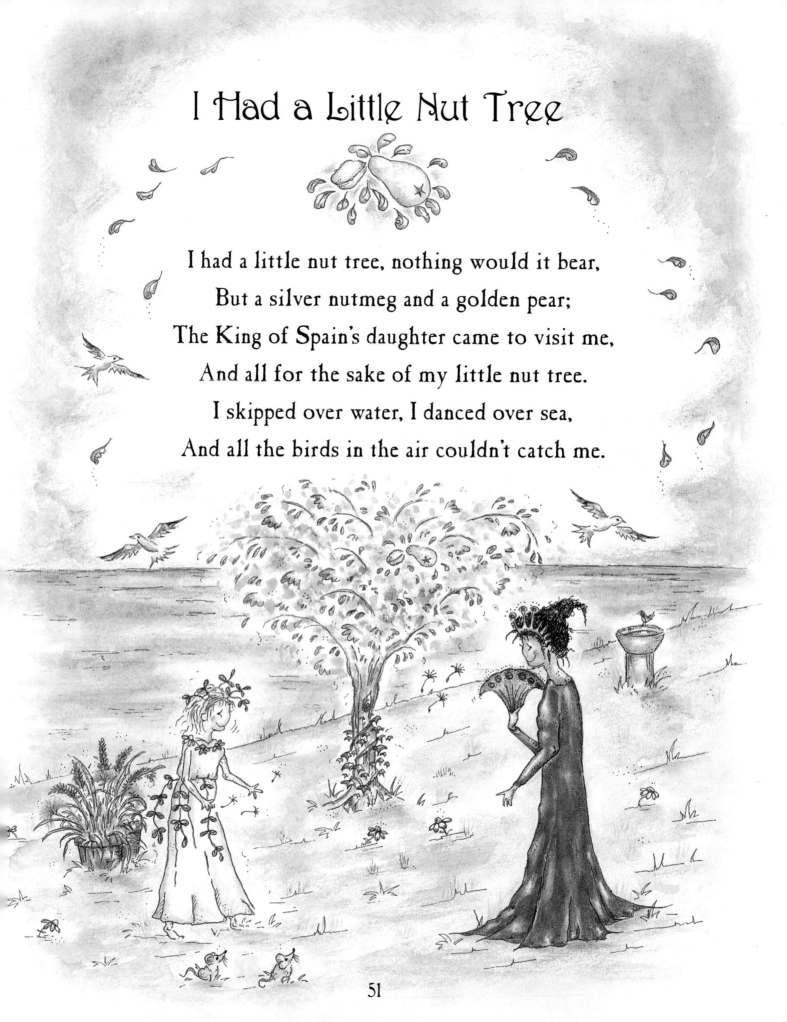

I had a little nut tree, nothing would it bear,
But a silver nutmeg and a golden pear;
The King of Spain's daughter came to visit me,
And all for the sake of my little nut tree.
I skipped over water, I danced over sea,
And all the birds in the air couldn't catch me.

Dingle Dangle Scarecrow

When all the cows were sleeping
And the sun had gone to bed,
Up jumped the scarecrow
And this is what he said:

I'm a dingle dangle scarecrow
With a flippy floppy hat!
I can shake my arms like this,
I can shake my legs like that!

DINGLE DANGLE

FLIPPY FLOPPY HAT

When the cows were in the meadow
And the pigeons in the loft,
Up jumped the scarecrow
And whispered very soft:
Chorus

SHAKE MY ARMS

SHAKE MY LEGS

When all the hens were roosting
And the moon behind a cloud,
Up jumped the scarecrow
And shouted very loud:
Chorus

MY BEST FRIEND

He cuddles me at bedtime,
And keeps me safe at night,
If I have a bad dream,
And wake up in a fright.

He is my constant playmate,
And often shares my tea,
He always lets me win at games,
And has a smile for me.

He shares in all my secrets,
And never shows surprise,
He listens to my problems,
With kindness in his eyes.

And when I'm feeling lonely,
On him I can depend,
He's more than just a teddy,
He is my best, best friend!

SOME TEDDY BEARS

Some teddy bears are tiny,
Some teddy bears are tall,
Some teddy bears are big and round,
And some teddy bears are small.

Some teddy bears are woolly,
Some teddy bears are rough,
Some teddy bears have shaggy fur,
And some are balls of fluff.

Some teddy bears look happy
Some teddy bears look sad,
Some teddy bears are very good,
And some teddy bears are bad.

But all teddy bears are loyal,
And all teddy bears are true,
And all teddy bears need lots of love
And hugs from me and you.

Oh Dear, What Can The Matter Be?

Oh dear, what can the matter be?
Dear, dear, what can the matter be?
Oh dear, what can the matter be?
Johnny's so long at the fair.

He promised he'd buy me a basket of posies,
A garland of lilies, a garland of roses,
A little straw hat to set off the blue ribbons
That tie up my bonny brown hair.

Oh dear, what can the matter be?
Dear, dear, what can the matter be?
Oh dear, what can the matter be?
Johnny's so long at the fair.

Five Little Peas

Clasp one hand around the other

Five little peas in a pea-pod pressed,

Raise thumbs, then rest of fingers

One grew, two grew, and so did all the rest.

Move hands apart slowly

They grew, and they grew, and they did not stop,

Clap!

Until one day the pod went... POP!

One Finger, One Thumb

One finger, one thumb, keep moving,
One finger, one thumb, keep moving,
One finger, one thumb, keep moving,
We'll all be merry and bright.

One finger, one thumb,
one arm, keep moving,
One finger, one thumb,
one arm, keep moving,
One finger, one thumb,
one arm, keep moving,
We'll all be merry and bright.

One finger, one thumb, one arm,
one leg, keep moving, etc

One finger, one thumb,
one arm, one leg, one nod
of the head, keep moving, etc.

This rhyme may be continued with other verses - stand up, sit down, turn around, etc.

LITTLE DOG LOST

"Brrr," shivered Scruffy. "It's cold tonight."

"Well, snuggle up closer to me," said his mom.

"It's not fair," Scruffy grumbled. "Why do we have to sleep outside in the cold? The cats are allowed to sleep inside, in nice warm baskets!"

"We're farm dogs, dear," said Mom. "We have to be tough, and work hard to earn our keep."

"I'd rather be a cat," mumbled Scruffy. "All they do is wash themselves, eat and sleep."

"We don't have such a bad life," said Mom. "Now stop feeling sorry for yourself, and get some rest. We've got a lot of work to do tomorrow."

The next day, Scruffy woke early and trotted down the lane for a walk. He ran through the grass, chasing rabbits, and sniffing at the flowers.

Now, usually when he got to the end of the lane he stopped and turned back. But today, he saw a big red van parked outside a house there. The back of the van was open, and Scruffy thought he would just climb inside and take a look.

The van was full of furniture. At the back was a big armchair with soft cushions. Scruffy clambered onto it. "I could doze all day, like a cat!" he told himself. He closed his eyes and before he knew it he had fallen fast asleep.

Scruffy awoke some time later with a sharp jolt.

"Oh, no, I fell asleep!" he groaned. "I'd better hurry back. We've got a busy day ahead!"

But then he saw that the truck doors were closed! He could hear voices outside.

"Oh, dear, I'll be in trouble if I get found in here," thought Scruffy, and he hid behind the chair.

The back of the truck opened and Scruffy peered out. Two men started unloading the furniture.

When Scruffy was sure that no one was looking, he crept out of the truck, but he was no longer in the countryside where he lived! He was in a big noisy town, full of buildings and cars.

Poor Scruffy had no idea where he was!

"The truck must have carried me away," thought Scruffy, feeling frightened.

All day long, Scruffy roamed around trying to find his way home, feeling cold, tired and hungry. At last, he lay down and began to howl miserably.

"What's the matter, pup?" he heard a man's kind voice say. "You look lost. Come home with me." Scruffy gave the man's hand a grateful lick, then jumped up and followed him home.

When they arrived at the man's house Scruffy sat on the doorstep, hoping the man might bring him some food out to eat. But the man said, "Come on in, you can't stay out there."

Scruffy followed the man in, and found a little poodle waiting to meet him. Scruffy stared at her in amazement. What had happened to her fur?

"You'd better take a bath before supper," said the man, looking at Scruffy's dirty white coat. The man washed him in a big tub, then brushed his tangled coat. Scruffy howled miserably. What had he done to deserve such punishment?

"Don't you like it?" asked the poodle, shyly.

"No, I don't," said Scruffy. "All this washing and cleaning is for cats!"

Next the man gave them supper — small bowls of dry pellets. Scruffy sniffed at them in disgust. He was used to chunks of meat and a nice big bone.

"This looks like cat food," said Scruffy, miserably.

After supper the poodle climbed into a big basket in the kitchen.

"I thought that belonged to a cat," said Scruffy. He tried sleeping in the basket but he was hot and uncomfortable. He missed counting the stars to help him fall asleep, and most of all he missed his mom.

"I want to go home," he cried, and big tears slipped down his nose.

The next day, the man put Scruffy on a lead and took him into town. He hated being dragged along, without being able to sniff at things.

Then, as they crossed the market place, Scruffy heard a familiar bark, and saw his mom's head hanging through the window of the farmer's truck! He started to howl, dragged the man over to where the truck was parked, then leapt up at the window barking excitedly. The farmer could hardly believe it was Scruffy — he had never seen him so clean! The man explained how he had found Scruffy, and the farmer thanked the man for taking such good care of him.

On the way back home, Scruffy told his mom all about his adventure and what had happened.

"I thought you had run away because you didn't like being a farm dog," she said gently.

"Oh, no, Mom," said Scruffy, quickly. "I love being a farm dog. I can't wait to get home to a nice big juicy bone and our little bed beneath the stars!"

Ten Little Fingers

I have ten little fingers,
And they all belong to me.
I can make them do things,

Would you like to see?
I can shut them up tight,
Or open them all wide.

Hold hands up

TEN LITTLE FINGERS

Waggle fingers

...ALL BELONG TO ME...

Clench fists

...SHUT THEM TIGHT...

Open hands wide

...OPEN THEM ALL WIDE

68

Put them all together,
Or make them all hide.
I can make them jump high;

I can make them jump low.
I can fold them quietly,
And hold them all just so.

Interlock fingers

PUT THEM ALTOGETHER

Place hands behind back

...MAKE THEM ALL HIDE

Move arms up and down

...JUMP HIGH/LOW

Put hands together in lap

HOLD THEM ALL JUST SO

69

I Saw A Ship A-Sailing

I saw a ship a-sailing,
A-sailing on the sea;
And, oh! but it was laden,
With pretty things for thee!
There were comfits in the cabin,
And apples in the hold;
The sails were made of silk,
And the masts were all of gold.
The four-and-twenty sailors
That stood between the decks,
Were four-and-twenty mice
With chains around their necks.
The captain was a duck
With a packet on his back;
And when the ship began to move,
The captain said, "Quack! Quack!"

If All The Seas

If all the seas were one sea

What a great sea that would be!

And if all the trees were one tree

What a great tree that would be!

And if all the axes were one axe

What a great axe that would be!

And if all the men were one man

What a great man he would be!

And if the great man took the great axe

And cut down the great tree

And let it fall into the great sea

What a splish splash that would be!

I Can ...

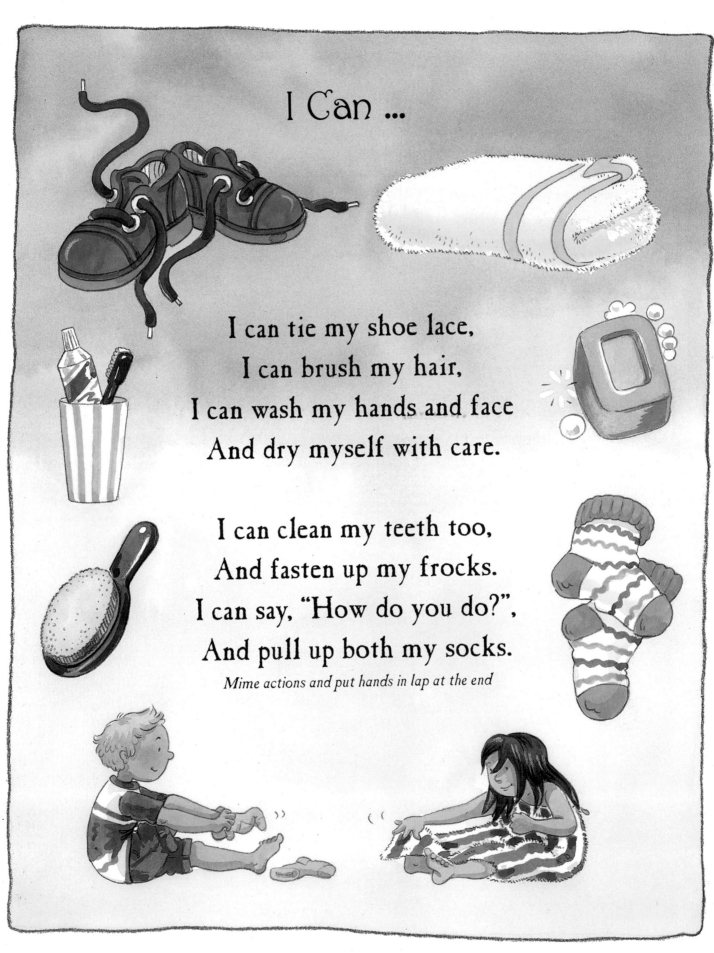

I can tie my shoe lace,
I can brush my hair,
I can wash my hands and face
And dry myself with care.

I can clean my teeth too,
And fasten up my frocks.
I can say, "How do you do?",
And pull up both my socks.

Mime actions and put hands in lap at the end

Shoes

Baby's shoes,

Mother's shoes,

Father's shoes,

Policeman's shoes,

GIANT'S SHOES!

Hold hands wider apart for each pair of shoes, and make voice get louder and louder

BABY'S SHOES   MOTHER'S SHOES   FATHER'S SHOES   GIANT'S SHOES!

As Small as a Mouse

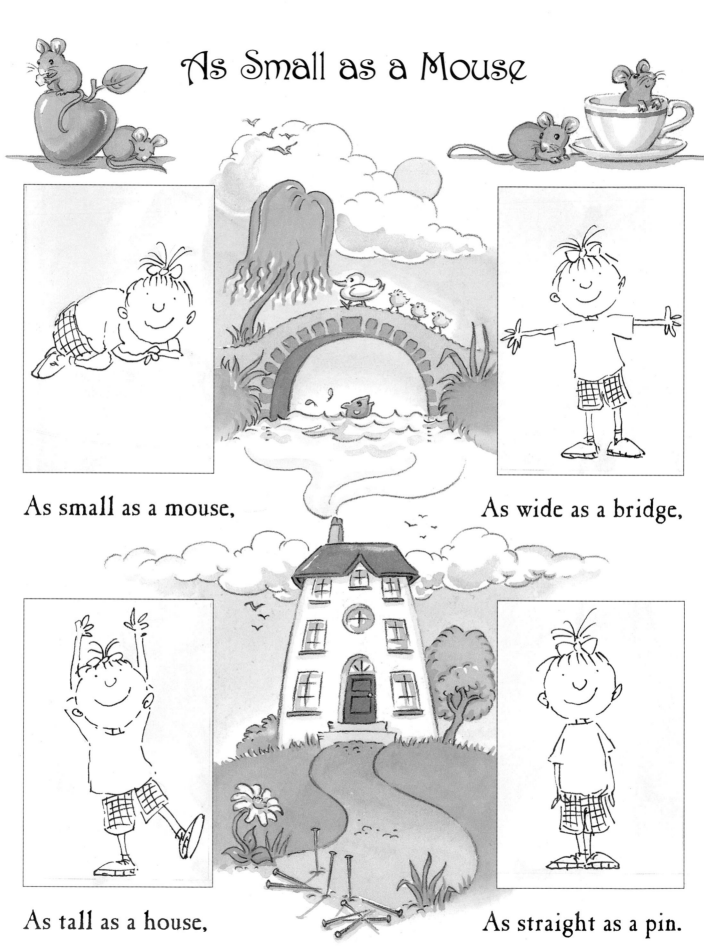

As small as a mouse,

As wide as a bridge,

As tall as a house,

As straight as a pin.

74

Slowly, Slowly

Slowly, slowly, very slowly
Creeps the garden snail.

Slowly, slowly, very slowly
Up the garden rail.

Quickly, quickly, very quickly
Runs the little mouse.

Quickly, quickly, very quickly
Round about the house.

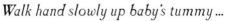

Walk hand slowly up baby's tummy ...

Tickle baby during second verse

THE BEAR
WILL HAVE TO GO

While Lucy slept in the shade of a tree, Cuthbert went for a walk into the woods and was soon quite lost. He had no idea which way was back, so he sat down and thought about what to do next.

When Lucy awoke, she looked around in surprise. Her teddy bear, Cuthbert, was missing. She thought someone had taken him, for she didn't know that when people are asleep their teddy bears like to go walking.

"Cuthbert!" she called. "Cuthbert, where are you?"

He wasn't very far away. Lucy soon found him sniffing at a clump of moss.

"There you are!" she sighed. "I thought I'd lost you. Where's your waistcoat?"

In fact, Lucy really had lost Cuthbert, for the bear she was now taking home was not a teddy bear at all, but a real baby bear cub! As they ran back through the woods, the bear in Lucy's arms kept very still. He stared straight ahead without blinking, and tried not to sneeze. Soon they were back in Lucy's bedroom. Lucy flung the bear on her bed, then went to run a bath.

"Time to escape!" thought the bear. He slid off the bed, pulling the covers after him. He ran over to the window and tried to climb up the curtains. They tore down and tumbled to a heap on the floor. Just then Lucy's mother came into the room. The bear froze. Then Lucy appeared.

"Look at this mess," said Lucy's mother. "You've been playing with that bear again. Please tidy up."

Lucy had no idea how her room had got in such a mess, but she tidied up, took the bear into the bathroom and put him on the edge of the tub.

"Don't fall in," she said, and went to fetch a towel. The bear jumped into the tub with a great splash. He waved his paws wildly sending sprays of soapy water across the room. When he heard footsteps, he froze and floated on his back in the water as if nothing was wrong. It was Lucy, followed by her mother. "Oh, Lucy! What a mess!"

"Cuthbert must have fallen in," cried Lucy, rubbing his wet fur with a towel.

"A teddy bear couldn't make all this mess on its own," said Lucy's mother. "Please clean it up."

Lucy looked carefully at Cuthbert. Something was different about him, but she just couldn't work out what it was.

That night, while Lucy slept, the bear tip-toed downstairs. He needed to get back to the woods where he belonged, but he was hungry. In the kitchen he found lots of food, and he had a feast.

When Lucy came down for a glass of milk she found him with food all over his paws. The bear froze. Then her mother appeared in the doorway.

"This is the last straw, Lucy," said her mother, crossly. "You have been very naughty today, and every time something happens you've got that bear with you. If there is any more bad behaviour, the bear will have to go."

When her mother had gone back upstairs, Lucy looked carefully at the bear.

"You're not Cuthbert are you?" she said. The bear looked back at her and blinked. Lucy gasped. "You're a real bear!"

Now all the mess made sense! Lucy could hardly believe she had made such a mistake. She stroked the bear gently and he licked her finger.

"I'd better get you back to the woods before there's any more trouble," she said. "And I'd better try to find the real Cuthbert."

So early next morning, before her parents were awake, she crept out of the house carrying the bear. Out in the woods she put the bear on the ground. He licked her hand and padded away.

Lucy was sad to see the little bear go. She wiped a tear from her eye as she turned away... and there at the foot of a tree sat her teddy bear, Cuthbert! Lucy picked him up and hugged him.

"Where have you been?" she asked. "You'll never guess the trouble I've been in. What have you been doing all night?"

Cuthbert said nothing. He just smiled. What had he been doing all night? Well, that's another story!

A Frog He Would A-Wooing Go

A frog he would a-wooing go,

Heigh ho! says Rowley,

Whether his mother would let him or no,

With a rowley, powley, gammon and spinach,

Heigh ho! says Anthony Rowley.

So off he set with his opera hat,

Heigh ho! says Rowley,

And on the way he met with a rat,

With a rowley, powley, gammon and spinach,

Heigh ho! says Anthony Rowley.

Pray, Mister Rat, will you go with me?
Heigh ho! says Rowley,
Kind Mistress Mousey for to see?
With a rowley, powley, gammon and spinach,
Heigh ho! says Anthony Rowley.

They came to the door of Mousey's hall,
Heigh ho! says Rowley,
They gave a loud knock and they gave a loud call.
With a rowley, powley, gammon and spinach,
Heigh ho! says Anthony Rowley.

Pray, Mistress Mouse, will you give us some beer?
Heigh ho! says Rowley,
For Froggy and I are fond of good cheer.
With a rowley, powley, gammon and spinach,
Heigh ho! says Anthony Rowley.

But while they were all a merry-making,
Heigh ho! says Rowley,
A cat and her kittens came tumbling in.
With a rowley, powley, gammon and spinach,
Heigh ho! says Anthony Rowley.

The cat she seized the rat by the crown,
Heigh ho! says Rowley,
The kittens they pulled the little mouse down.
With a rowley, powley, gammon and spinach,
Heigh ho! says Anthony Rowley.

This put Mister Frog in a terrible fright.
Heigh ho! says Rowley,
He took up his hat and he wished them goodnight.
With a rowley, powley, gammon and spinach,
Heigh ho! says Anthony Rowley.

MIDNIGHT FUN

Just as midnight's striking,
When everyone's asleep,
Teddies yawn and stretch and shake,
And out of warm beds creep.

They sneak out from their houses,
And gather in the dark,
Then skip along the empty streets,
Heading for the park.

And there beneath the moonlight,
They tumble down the slides,
They swoosh up high upon the swings,
And play on all the rides.

And when the sun comes peeping,
They rush home to their beds,
And snuggle down as children wake,
To cuddle with their teds!

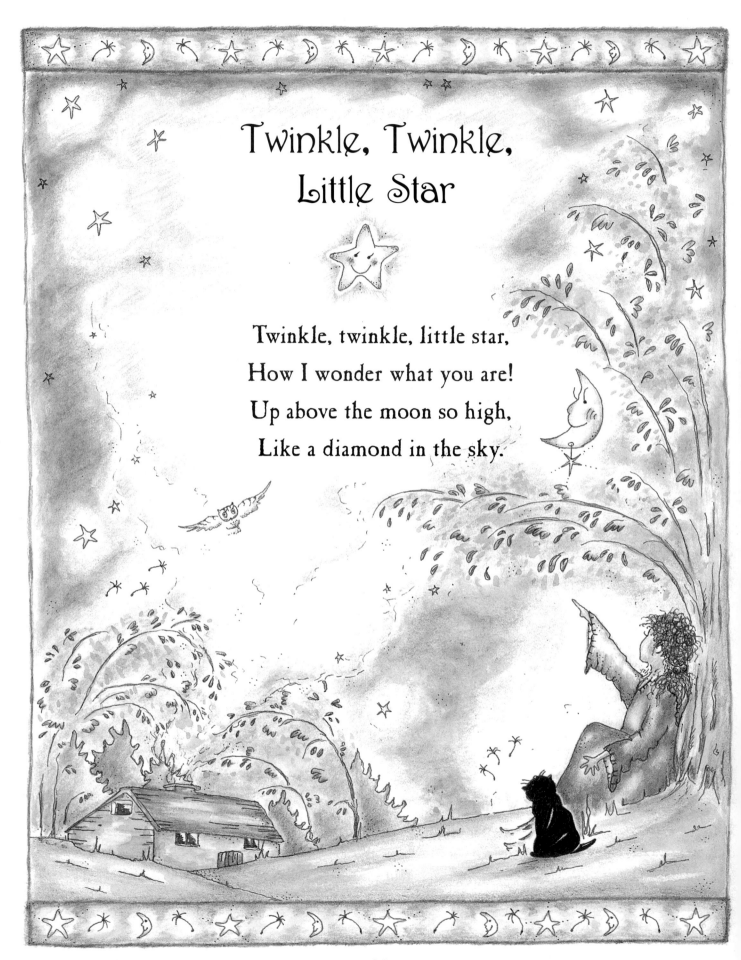

Twinkle, Twinkle, Little Star

Twinkle, twinkle, little star,
How I wonder what you are!
Up above the moon so high,
Like a diamond in the sky.

Ride a Cock-Horse

Ride a cock-horse to Banbury Cross,

To see a fine lady upon a white horse,

With rings on her fingers and bells on her toes

She shall have music wherever she goes.

Little Cottage in the Wood

Make roof with hands

LITTLE COTTAGE

Look through hands

MAN BY THE WINDOW

Hold up fingers

RABBIT RUNNING

Knock fist in air

KNOCKING AT DOOR

Little cottage in the wood,
Little old man by the window stood,
Saw a rabbit running by,
Knocking at the door.
"Help me! Help me! Help me!" he said,
"Before the huntsman shoots me dead."
"Come little rabbit, come inside,
Safe with me abide."

Wave arms up and down

HELP ME!

Point with one finger

HUNTSMAN SHOOTS

Beckon with same finger

COME INSIDE

Stroke hand (rabbit)

SAFE WITH ME

THE LITTLEST PIG

Little Pig had a secret. He snuggled down in the warm hay with his brothers and sisters, looked up at the dark sky twinkling with stars, and smiled a secret smile to himself. Maybe it wasn't so bad being the littlest pig after all...

Not so long ago, Little Pig had been feeling quite fed up. He was the youngest and by far the smallest pig in the family. He had five brothers and five sisters and they were all much bigger and fatter than he was. The farmer's wife called him Runt, as he was the smallest pig of the litter.

"I don't suppose little Runt will come to much," she told her friend Daisy, as they stopped by to bring the piglets some fresh hay.

95

His brothers and sisters teased him terribly. "Poor little Runtie," they said to him, giggling. "You must be the smallest pig in the world!"

"Leave me alone!" said Little Pig, and he crept off to the corner of the pig pen, where he curled into a ball, and started to cry. "If you weren't all so greedy, and let me have some food, maybe I'd be bigger!" he mumbled, sadly.

Every feeding time was the same — the others
all pushed and shoved, and shunted Little Pig out
of the way, until all that was left were the scraps.
He would never grow bigger at this rate.

Then one day Little Pig made an important
discovery. He was hiding in the corner of the pen,
as usual, when he spied a little hole in the fence
tucked away behind the feeding trough.

"I think I could fit through there!" thought Little Pig, excitedly.

He waited all day until it was time for bed, and then, when he was sure that all of his brothers and sisters were fast asleep, he wriggled through the hole. Suddenly he was outside, free to go wherever he pleased. And what an adventure he had!

First, he ran to the henhouse and gobbled up the bowls of grain. Then he ran to the field, slipped under the fence, and crunched up Donkey's carrots.

He ran into the vegetable patch and munched a whole row of cabbages. What a wonderful feast! Then, when his little belly was full to bursting, he headed for home. On the way he stopped by the hedgerow. What was that lovely smell? He rooted around until he found where it was coming from – it was a bank of wild strawberries.

Little Pig had never tasted anything so delicious. "Tomorrow night, I'll start with these!" he promised himself as he trotted back home to the pig pen.

Quietly he wriggled back through the hole, and soon fell fast asleep snuggled up to his mother, smiling contentedly.

Night after night Little Pig continued his tasty adventures, creeping out through the hole when the others were sleeping. He no longer minded when they pushed him out of the way at feeding time, as he knew a much better feast awaited him outside. Sometimes he would find the farm dog's bowl filled with scraps from the farmer's supper, or buckets of oats ready for the horses. "Yum, yum — piggy porridge!" he would giggle, as he gobbled it up.

But as the days and weeks went by, and Little Pig grew bigger and fatter, it was more of a squeeze to wriggle through the hole each night.

Little Pig knew that soon he would no longer be able to fit through the hole, but by then he would be big enough to stand up to his brothers and sisters. And for now he was enjoying his secret!

The Wheels on the Bus

The wheels on the bus go round and round,
Round and round, round and round,
The wheels on the bus
go round and round,
All day long.

The wipers on
the bus go swish,
swish, swish, etc.

The horn on the bus
goes beep! beep! beep! etc.

*Move fists in a
circular motion*

ROUND AND ROUND

*Waggle both extended
index fingers*

SWISH, SWISH, SWISH

Pretend to press a horn

BEEP! BEEP! BEEP!

*Pat thumb on rest of
extended fingers*

CHAT, CHAT, CHAT

The people on the bus go chat, chat, chat, etc.

The children on the bus bump up and down, etc.

The babies on the bus go "WAAH! WAAH! WAAH!", etc.

The grannies on the bus go knit, knit, knit, etc.

The wheels on the bus go round and round, All day long.

Bump up and down on chair

BUMP UP AND DOWN

Make 'waah' sound with hands around mouth

WAAH! WAAH! WAAH!

Pretend to knit with extended index fingers

KNIT, KNIT, KNIT

Repeat first action

ROUND AND ROUND

Ten Green Bottles

Ten green bottles, standing on a wall,

Ten green bottles, standing on a wall,

And if one green bottle should accidentally fall,

There'd be nine green bottles, standing on a wall.

(continue with nine green bottles etc...)

Frère Jacques

Frère Jacques, Frère Jacques,

Dormez-vous, dormez-vous?

Sonnez les matines, sonnez les matines,

Ding, dang, dong, ding, dang, dong.

ELEPHANTS NEVER FORGET

I woke up this morning, astounded,
To find my long trunk in a knot!
I know it must be to remind me
To remember something I've forgot!

But though I've been thinking all morning
I haven't remembered it yet.
Still I'm sure I will think of it soon,
Because elephants never forget!

ITCHY SPOTS

Poor Monkey was wriggling
And jiggling around,
Scratching and making
A chattering sound:

Then along came a bear
In a bit of a stew —
"I've got such a bad itch,
I don't know what to do!

"They're driving me mad,
Someone help me please –
I have to get rid of
These terrible fleas!"

It's right in a spot
I can't reach with my paws.
So why not scratch my back,
And I will scratch yours!"

One Man Went To Mow

One man went to mow, went to mow a meadow,
One man and his dog, Spot,
Went to mow a meadow.

Two men went to mow, went to mow a meadow,
Two men, one man and his dog, Spot,
Went to mow a meadow.

Three men went to mow, went to mow a meadow,
Three men, two men, one man and his dog, Spot,
Went to mow a meadow.

Four men went to mow, went to mow a meadow,
Four men, three men, two men, one man and his dog, Spot,
Went to mow a meadow.

Five men went to mow, went to mow a meadow,
Five men, four men, three men, two men,
one man and his dog, Spot,
Went to mow a meadow.

I'm a Little Teapot

SHORT

AND STOUT

HANDLE

SPOUT

I'm a little teapot
short and stout,
Here's my handle,
here's my spout,
When I get my
steam up hear me shout,
Tip me up
and pour me out.

STEAM UP

SHOUT

TIP

POUR

110

Okey Cokey

You put your left arm in, your left arm out,
In, out, in, out, you shake it all about,
You do the okey cokey, and you turn around,
And that's what it's all about.

Oh, the okey cokey,
Oh, the okey cokey,
Oh, the okey cokey,
Knees bend, arms stretch,
Ra, ra, ra!

Rhyme continues with right arm, left leg, right leg, whole self.

LEFT ARM IN...

LEFT ARM OUT...

SHAKE IT ALL ABOUT...

TURN AROUND...

KNEES BEND, ARM STRETCH

WOBBLY BEAR

Mr and Mrs Puppety owned an old-fashioned toy shop. They made toys by hand in a room at the back of the shop. But they were getting old and their eyesight was bad.

"It's time we got an apprentice toymaker," said Mr Puppety to his wife. They soon found a young lad called Tom to work for them. He worked hard and carefully. He spent his first week making a teddy bear. When he had finished he showed the bear to Mr and Mrs Puppety.

"He looks very cuddly," said Mrs Puppety.

Tom was pleased that they liked his bear and he went off home whistling happily.

"He is a lovely bear," said Mr Puppety, "but his head is a bit wobbly."

"I know," said his wife, "but it's Tom's first try. Let's just put him up there on the shelf with the other teddy bears."

That night Wobbly Bear sat on the shelf and started to cry. He had heard what Mr and Mrs Puppety had said about him.

"What's wrong?" asked Brown Bear, who was sitting next to him.

"My head is on wobbly," sobbed Wobbly Bear.

"Does it hurt?" asked Brown Bear.

"No," replied Wobbly Bear.

"Then why are you crying?" asked Brown Bear.

"Because nobody will want to buy a wobbly bear. I'll be left in this shop forever and nobody will ever take me home and love me," he cried.

"Don't worry," said Brown Bear. "We've all got our faults, and you look fine to me. Just try your best to look cute and cuddly and you'll soon have someone to love you." This made Wobbly Bear feel much happier and he soon fell fast asleep.

The next day the shop was full of people, but nobody paid any attention to Wobbly Bear. Then a little boy looked up at the shelf and cried, "Oh, what a lovely bear. Can I have that one, Daddy?"

Wobbly Bear's heart lifted as the little boy's daddy reached up to his shelf. But he picked up Brown Bear instead and handed him to the little boy. Wobbly Bear felt sadder than ever. Nobody wanted him. All of his new friends would get sold and leave the shop, but he would be left on the shelf gathering dust. Poor old Wobbly Bear!

Now, Mr and Mrs Puppety had a little grand-daughter called Jessie who loved to visit the shop and play with the toys. All the toys loved her because she was gentle and kind. It so happened that the next time she came to visit it was her birthday, and her grandparents told her she could choose any toy she wanted as her present.

"I know she won't choose me," thought Wobbly Bear sadly. "Not with all these other beautiful toys to choose from."

117

But to Wobbly's amazement, Jessie looked up and pointed at his shelf and said, "I'd like that wobbly bear please. No one else will have a bear quite like him."

Mr Puppety smiled and gave Wobbly to Jessie. She hugged and kissed him, and Wobbly felt so happy he almost cried. She took him home and put a smart red bow around his neck ready for her birthday party. He felt very proud indeed.

Soon the other children arrived, each carrying their teddy bears under their arms.

Wobbly Bear could not believe his eyes when he saw the little boy with his friend Brown Bear!

"I'm having a teddy bears' picnic," Jessie explained to him, hugging him tight. All of the children and the bears had a wonderful time, especially Wobbly. He had found a lovely home, met his old friend and made lots of new ones.

"See, I told you not to worry," said Brown Bear.

"I know," said Wobbly. "And I never will again."

The Beehive

Here is the beehive.
Where are the bees?
Hidden away where nobody sees.
Soon they come
creeping out of the hive,
One, two, three, four, five!

*Fold one hand over the
other to make hive*

Slowly bring out thumb...

*...followed by the other
fingers, one by one*

Suddenly tickle child!

BEEHIVE

THEY COME CREEPING...

...THREE, FOUR...

...FIVE!

Dancing Round the Maypole

Dancing round the maypole,
Dancing all the day,
Dancing round the maypole,
On the first of May,
Dancing round the maypole,
What a merry bunch,
Dancing round the maypole,
Till it's time for lunch.

Dancing round the maypole,

Shouting out with glee,

Dancing round the maypole,

Till it's time for tea.

Dancing round the maypole,

Blue and white and red,

Dancing round the maypole,

Till it's time for bed.

TEDDY BEAR'S PICNIC

Little Bear brought chocolate cake,
Raggy Bear brought honey,
Baby Bear brought ice-cream,
With butterscotch all runny!

Tough Old Ted brought cinnamon bunss,
Silky Bear brought jello,
Shaggy Bear brought cookies and
Egg sandwiches all yellow!

Woolly Bear brought pecan pie,
Tiny Ted brought candy,
Mrs Bear brought little plates,
She thought would come in handy.

Off they set into the woods,
A sunny spot they found,
And had a teddies picnic,
As they shared the goodies round!

Row, Row, Row Your Boat

Row, row, row your boat,
Gently down the stream,
Merrily, merrily, merrily, merrily,
Life is but a dream.

Mime rowing action throughout...

Round About There

Round about there,
Sat a little hare,
A cat came and
chased him,
Right up there!

Circle child's palm with finger

ROUND ABOUT THERE

Walk fingers up arm

A CAT CAME AND CHASED HIM

Tickle!

RIGHT UP THERE!

Five Fat Sausages

Hold up five fingers

FIVE FAT SAUSAGES

Clap!

...ONE WENT BANG!

Hold up four fingers

FOUR FAT SAUSAGES

Clap!

...ONE WENT BANG!

Five fat sausages frying in a pan,
All of a sudden one went 'BANG!'
Four fat sausages, etc.
Three fat sausages, etc.
Two fat sausages, etc.
One fat sausage frying in a pan,
All of a sudden it went 'BANG!'
and there were NO sausages left!

Continue until one finger left

ONE FAT SAUSAGE

Clap!

...IT WENT BANG!

NO SAUSAGES!

Two Fat Gentlemen

Two fat gentlemen
met in a lane,
Bowed most politely,
bowed once again.
How do you do?
How do you do?
How do you do again?

Two thin ladies met in a lane, etc.
Two tall policemen met in a lane, etc.
Two little schoolboys met in a lane, etc.
Two little babies met in a lane, etc.

Repeat actions for other fingers: two thin ladies = index fingers, etc.

*Hold out fists
with thumbs raised*

TWO FAT GENTLEMEN...

Bend each thumb in turn

BOWED MOST POLITELY

*Wiggle each
thumb in turn*

HOW DO YOU DO?

Wiggle thumbs together

HOW DO YOU DO AGAIN?

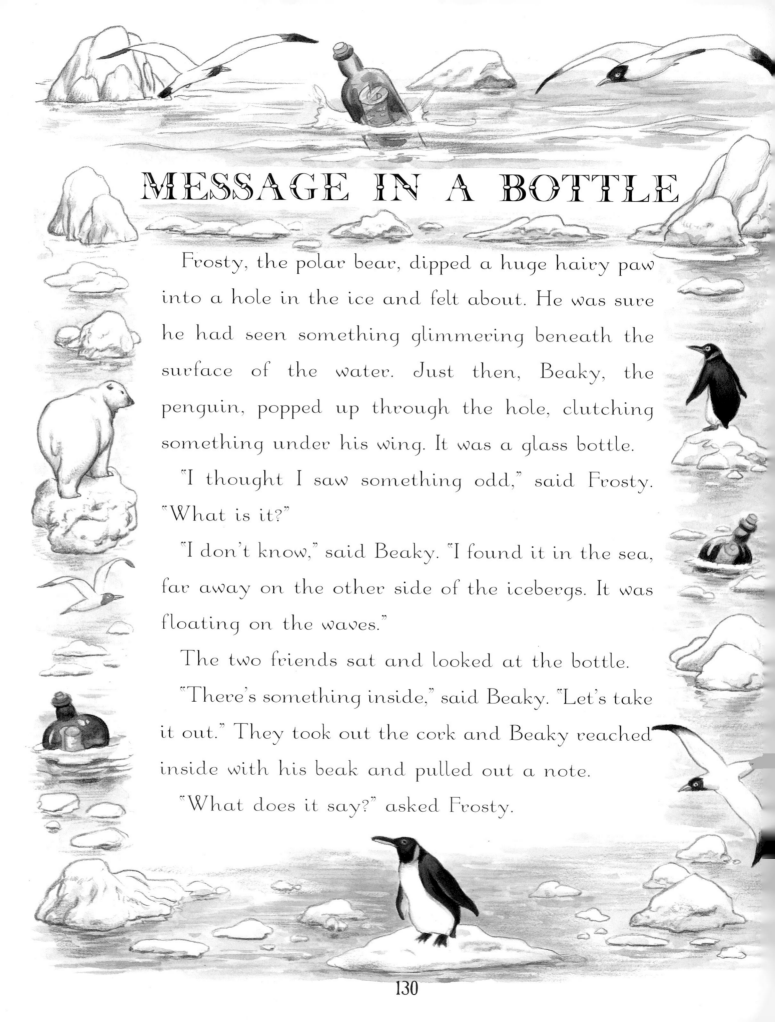

MESSAGE IN A BOTTLE

Frosty, the polar bear, dipped a huge hairy paw into a hole in the ice and felt about. He was sure he had seen something glimmering beneath the surface of the water. Just then, Beaky, the penguin, popped up through the hole, clutching something under his wing. It was a glass bottle.

"I thought I saw something odd," said Frosty. "What is it?"

"I don't know," said Beaky. "I found it in the sea, far away on the other side of the icebergs. It was floating on the waves."

The two friends sat and looked at the bottle.

"There's something inside," said Beaky. "Let's take it out." They took out the cork and Beaky reached inside with his beak and pulled out a note.

"What does it say?" asked Frosty.

130

Beaky peered closely at the note.

"It says: 'Help. I am stranded on a desert island. My boat is broken. It is very hot. Love Browny, the bear,'" read Beaky. "There's a map on the other side. Do you think we should help?"

"Of course we should," said Frosty. "It sounds like one of my cousins is in trouble. Anyway, it will be a great adventure! I've always wanted to know what hot feels like!"

The two friends studied the map carefully, then set off across the ice and snow until they reached the sea. They turned and waved goodbye to their chilly home, dove into the icy water and started to swim south in the direction of the desert island. After a while, Frosty began to feel tired. He had never swum so far away from home before.

"Let's rest a moment," said Beaky, and they flipped over in the water and lay floating along on their backs.

"Do you think it's much further?" asked Frosty.

"Oh, yes, much further," said Beaky. "The water has not even begun to get warm yet. By the time we get there it will be like taking a hot bath."

"I've never had one of those!" said Frosty, excitedly. "Will I like it?"

"I'm not sure," said Beaky.

So the two friends carried on swimming towards the sunshine. Gradually the water grew warmer and warmer. Frosty started to laugh.

"My skin's all nice and tingly," he chuckled.

On and on they swam. The bright sun beat down on their heads. By now Frosty was puffing and panting with every stroke.

"I think I must be feeling hot," he said. "I don't think I can swim much further!

"You don't have to!" said Beaky, pointing with his wing. "There's the island!"

On the shore, Browny was jumping up and down with excitement and waving his paws.

"You found me!" he cried. "Imagine my little bottle floating all the way to the North Pole!"

"Imagine me swimming all the way here from the North Pole!" panted Frosty, as he staggered out of the sea and collapsed in a heap on the hot sand. "I'm exhausted!"

Browny led his rescuers to the shelter of a cave he had found nearby, and they rested there until they recovered. As night fell, Browny built a fire on the beach, and they sat telling stories. He told them all about finding a little boat and setting sail across the sea, and how his boat had been shipwrecked.

"I thought I would be stranded here for ever!" Browny said. "And I want to go home!"

"Don't worry," said Frosty. "We'll get you home. But first let's get a good night's rest."

The next morning the three friends had great fun playing on the beach.

"I'm not sure I like hot, though," said Frosty, "it makes me tired and uncomfortable. And this sand stuff gets everywhere!" The others laughed.

"Let's be on our way then," said Beaky.

And so they set back off across the ocean, pulling Browny along on a raft he'd made, as he wasn't a good swimmer like the others. It was another long, hard journey, but when they finally reached Browny's home and saw how happy he was to be back there, they knew it was worth it.

"Promise you'll come and visit me again!" cried Browny, as the others waved goodbye and set off once more for their chilly home.

"We will!" cried Frosty. "But not if you're somewhere hot. I can't wait to get home for a good slide on the ice!"

The Ostrich

Here is the ostrich
straight and tall,

Nodding his head
above us all.

Here is the hedgehog
prickly and small,

Rolling himself
into a ball.

Hold up arm

OSTRICH

Nod hand in air

NODS HIS HEAD

Interlace fingers

HEDGEHOG

Close hands in a ball

HEDGEHOG IN BALL

Here is the spider scuttling around,
Treading so lightly on the ground.

Here are the birds that fly so high,
Spreading their wings across the sky.

Here are the children fast asleep,
And in the night the owls do peep,

Wriggle fingers

SPIDER

Lock thumbs together

BIRDS

Pretend to sleep

CHILDREN ASLEEP

Make rings around eyes

OWLS

Simple Simon

Simple Simon met a pieman
Going to the fair,
Says Simple Simon to the pieman
"Let me taste your ware."
Says the pieman to Simple Simon,
"Show me first your penny."
Says Simple Simon to the pieman,
"Indeed I have not any."

Simple Simon went a-fishing
For to catch a whale;
But all the water he had got
Was in his mother's pail.

HIGH JUMP

The Shrew said to the Kangaroo,
"I can jump as high as you!"
Laughed Kanga, "How can that be true
Of one so small, please tell me, do!"

Said Shrew, "I'll show you, then you'll see,
I'll jump so high, I'll reach that tree!
But first of all you must agree,
To show your jumping skills to me!"

Then Kanga bounced into the air,
So busy he was unaware
That Shrew was clinging to his hair
To reach the treetop – most unfair!

Back Kanga landed on the ground,
"Your turn," he said, and spun around.
"Up here!" called Shrew, a distant sound.
"Well," said Kanga, "I'll be bound!"

Peter Works With One Hammer

Peter works with one hammer,
one hammer, one hammer,
Peter works with one hammer,
this fine day.

Peter works with two hammers,
two hammers, two hammers,
Peter works with two hammers,
this fine day.

Peter works with three hammers, etc.
Peter works with four hammers, etc.
Peter works with five hammers, etc.

Bang one fist on knee in rhythm

ONE HAMMER

Bang two fists on knees

TWO HAMMERS

Bang two fists, tap one foot

THREE HAMMERS

Bang two fists, tap two feet

FOUR HAMMERS

Peter's very tired now,
tired now, tired now,
Peter's very tired now,
this fine day.

Peter's going to sleep now,
sleep now, sleep now,
Peter's going to sleep now,
this fine day.

Peter's waking up now,
up now, up now,
Peter's waking up now,
this fine day.

Bang two fists, tap two feet and nod head

FIVE HAMMERS

Rub eyes and stretch as if yawning

TIRED NOW

Pretend to sleep

GOING TO SLEEP

Pretend to wake and stretch

WAKING UP

Little Miss Muffet

Little Miss Muffet
Sat on a tuffet,
Eating her curds and whey;
There came a big spider,
Who sat down beside her,
And frightened Miss Muffet away.

Wee Willie Winkie

Wee Willie Winkie runs through the town,
Upstairs and downstairs in his nightgown,
Rapping at the windows, crying through the locks,
"Are the children in their beds,
It's past eight o'clock?"

LAZY TEDDY

There was nothing Lazy Teddy liked more than to be tucked up snug and warm in Joshua's bed. Every morning the alarm clock would ring and Joshua would leap out of bed and fling open the curtains. "I love mornings!" he'd say, stretching his arms up high as the sun poured in through the window. "You're crazy!" Teddy would mutter, and he'd burrow down beneath the quilt to the bottom of the bed, where he'd spend the rest of the morning snoozing happily.

"Come out and play, you lazy bear," Joshua would call. But Lazy Teddy wouldn't budge. He would just snore even louder.

Joshua wished that Teddy would be more lively, like his other friends' bears. He loved having adventures, but they would be even better if Teddy would share them with him.

One evening, Joshua decided to have a talk with Teddy before they went to bed. He told him all about the fishing trip he'd been on that day with his friends and their teddy bears.

"It was lots of fun, Teddy. I wish you'd been there. It really is time you stopped being such a lazybones. Tomorrow is my birthday, and I'm having a party. There will be games, and presents and ice-cream. Please promise you'll come?"

"It does sound like fun," said Teddy. "Okay, I promise. I'll get up just this once."

The next morning, Joshua was up bright and early. "Yippee, it's my birthday today!" he yelled, dancing round the room. He pulled the covers off his bed. "Come on, Teddy, time to get up!"

"Just five more minutes!" groaned Teddy, and he rolled over and fell straight back to sleep. When Joshua came back up to his room after breakfast, Teddy still wasn't up. Well, by now Joshua was getting quite cross with Teddy. He reached over and poked him in the tummy. Teddy opened one eye and growled. "Wake up, Teddy! You promised, remember?" said Joshua.

Teddy yawned. "Oh, if I must!" he said, and muttering and grumbling he climbed out of bed. He washed his face and paws, brushed his teeth and put on his best red vest.

"There, I'm ready!" he said.

"Good," said Joshua. "About time too!"

Just then the doorbell rang, and Joshua ran to answer it. "I'll come and fetch you in a minute," he said to Teddy. But when he returned there was no sign of Teddy, just a gentle snoring coming from the bottom of the bed.

Joshua was so cross and upset with Lazy Teddy, that he decided to leave him right where he was.

"He'll just have to miss the party!" he said. Deep down though, he was hurt that Teddy wouldn't keep his promise.

Joshua enjoyed his party, although he wished that Teddy had been there. That night when he got into bed, he lay crying quietly into his pillow.

Teddy lay awake in the dark, listening. He knew Joshua was crying because he had let him down, and he felt very ashamed of himself.

"I'm sorry!" whispered Lazy Teddy, and he snuggled up to Joshua and stroked him with a paw until he fell asleep.

The next morning when the alarm clock rang, Joshua leapt out of bed, as usual. But what was this? Teddy had leapt out of bed too, and was stretching his paws up high. Joshua looked at him in amazement.

"What are we doing today, then?" asked Teddy.

"G...g...going for a picnic," stammered Joshua, in surprise. "Are you coming?"

"Of course," said Teddy. And from that day on, Teddy was up bright and early every day, ready to enjoy another day of adventures with Joshua, and he never let him down again.

Here's a Ball for Baby

Here's a ball for baby,
Big and fat and round.

Here is baby's hammer,
See how it can pound.

Here are baby's soldiers,
Standing in a row.

Here is baby's music,
Clapping, clapping so.

Make ball with hands

BALL

Tap fist against knee

HAMMER

Show ten fingers

SOLDIERS

Clap hands

CLAPPING

Here is baby's trumpet,
TOOTLE-TOOTLE-OO!

Here's the way the baby
Plays at peek-a-boo.

Here's a big umbrella,
To keep the baby dry.

Here is baby's cradle,
Rock-a-baby-bye.

Blow through fist

TRUMPET

Hands up to eyes

PEEK-A-BOO

Pretend to hold umbrella

UMBRELLA

Rock hands in cradle

CRADLE

Goosey, Goosey Gander

Goosey, goosey, gander,

Whither shall I wander?

Upstairs and downstairs,

And in my lady's chamber.

There I met an old man

Who would not say his prayers.

I took him by the left leg

And threw him down the stairs.

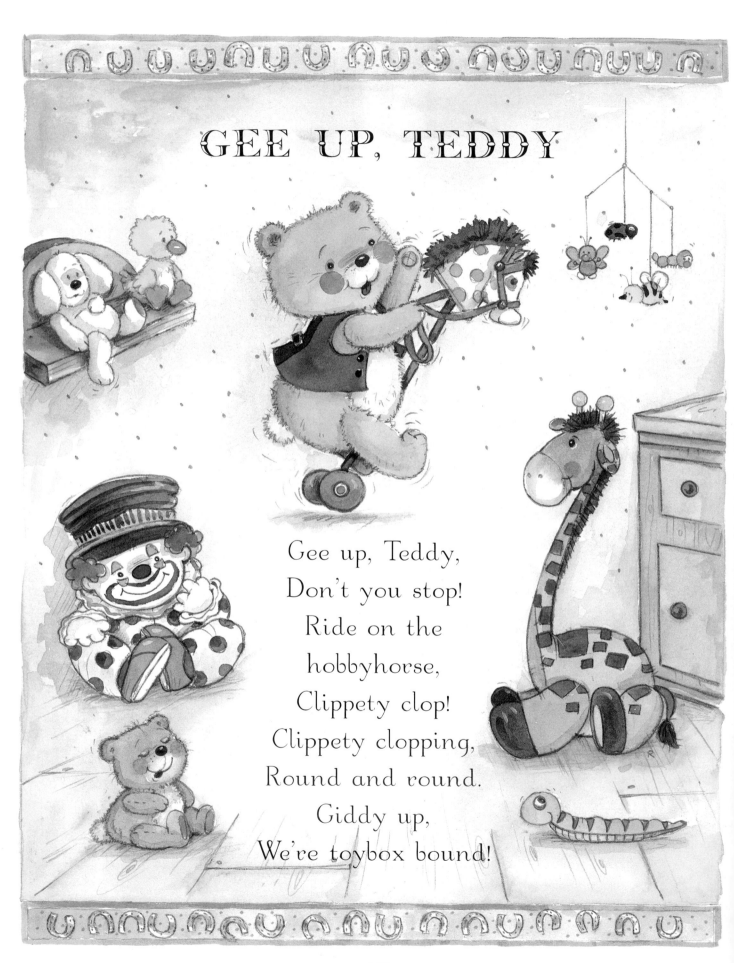

GEE UP, TEDDY

Gee up, Teddy,
Don't you stop!
Ride on the
hobbyhorse,
Clippety clop!
Clippety clopping,
Round and round.
Giddy up,
We're toybox bound!

THREE TEDS IN A TUB

Rub-a-dub, dub,
Three teds in a tub,
Sailing across the sea!
But the rumble of tums,
And the smell of hot buns,
Will bring them back home for tea!

Pat-A-Cake

Pat-a-cake, pat-a-cake,
baker's man,

Bake me a cake,
as fast as you can.

Pat it and prick it and
mark it with B,

And put it in the oven
for Baby and me.

Clap in rhythm

Pat and 'prick' palm

Trace the letter B on palm

Put cake in oven

PAT-A-CAKE

PAT IT, PRICK IT

MARK IT WITH B

PUT IN THE OVEN

Head, Shoulders, Knees and Toes

Head, shoulders, knees
and toes, knees and toes,
Head, shoulders, knees
and toes, knees and toes,
And eyes and ears
and mouth and nose.
Head, shoulders, knees
and toes, knees and toes.

Sing slow at first, then faster.

The Apple Tree

Here is the tree with leaves so green.
Here are the apples that hang between.
When the wind blows the apples fall.
Here is a basket to gather them all.

Make tree with arms

Make fists

Wave arms then let fists fall suddenly

Link hands to make a basket

HERE IS THE TREE...

HERE ARE THE APPLES...

...THE APPLES FALL

HERE IS THE BASKET...

The Cherry Tree

Once I found a cherry stone,
I put it in the ground,
And when I came to look at it,
A tiny shoot I found.

The shoot grew up and up each day,
And soon became a tree.
I picked the rosy cherries then,
And ate them for my tea.

Make hole with one hand and pretend to plant stone	*Slowly push finger up through 'hole'*	*Push hand up through hole, and hold wrist*	*Pretend to pick cherry from each finger and eat!*
ONCE I FOUND...	...A TINY SHOOT I FOUND	...SOON BECAME A TREE	...ATE THEM FOR MY TEA

Knick Knack Paddy Whack

This old man, he played one,
He played knick knack on my drum.
With a knick knack paddy whack, give a dog a bone,
This old man went rolling home.

This old man, he played two,
He played knick knack on my shoe.
With a knick knack paddy whack, give a dog a bone,
This old man went rolling home.

This old man, he played three,

He played knick knack on my knee.

With a knick knack paddy whack, give a dog a bone,

This old man went rolling home.

This old man, he played four,

He played knick knack on my door.

With a knick knack paddy whack, give a dog a bone,

This old man went rolling home.

This old man, he played five,

He played knick knack on my hive.

With a knick knack paddy whack, give a dog a bone,

This old man went rolling home.

WHALE SONG

"Oh, what a beautiful morning!" sang Flippy, the whale, as streaks of sunlight filtered down through the clear blue ocean. He swam to and fro, twirled around, then whooshed up through the waves, and jumped clear of the water in a perfect pirouette.

Flippy loved to sing and dance. The trouble was, although he was a very graceful dancer, his singing was terrible. His big mouth would open wide, as he boomed out song after song — but none of them were in tune! The dreadful sound echoed through the ocean for miles, sending all the fish and other ocean creatures diving into the rocks and reefs for cover, as the waters shook around them. It was always worse when the sun shone, as the bright warm sun made Flippy want to sing and dance with happiness. It had got so bad that the other creatures had begun to pray for dull skies and rain.

"Something has got to be done!" complained Wobble, the jellyfish. "Flippy's booming voice makes me quiver and shake so much that I can't see where I'm going!"

"Well, I know where I'm going," said Snappy, the lobster. "As far away as possible. My head is splitting from Flippy's awful wailing."

"Someone will have to tell Flippy not to sing anymore," said Sparky, the stingray.

"But it will hurt his feelings," said Wobble.

"Not as much as his singing hurts my ears!" snapped Snappy.

And so they decided that Sparky would tell Flippy the next day that they did not want him to sing any more songs. Wobble was right. Flippy was very upset when he heard that the others did not like his singing. He cried big, salty tears.

"I was only trying to enjoy myself!" he sobbed.
"I didn't realise I was upsetting everyone else."

"There, there," said Sparky, wishing he had not
been chosen to give the little whale the bad news.
"You can still enjoy dancing."

"It's not the same without music," said Flippy,
miserably. "You can't get the rhythm." And he
swam off into the deep waters, saying he wanted
to be alone for a while.

As Flippy lay on the bottom of the ocean floor, feeling very sorry for himself, a beautiful sound came floating through the water from far away in the distance. It sounded like someone singing. Flippy wanted to know who was making such a lovely sound, so with a flick of his big tail, he set off in the direction it was coming from.

As he got closer, he could hear a soft voice singing a beautiful melody. Peering out from behind a big rock, he saw that the voice belonged to a little octopus, who was shuffling and swaying about on the ocean floor. His legs seemed to be going in all directions, as he stumbled and tripped along.

Then he tried to spin around, but his legs got tangled and he crashed to the ground in a heap.

"Oh, dear," said Leggy, the octopus. "I seem to have eight left feet!"

Flippy looked out shyly from behind the rock.

"What are you trying to do?" he asked.

The little octopus looked rather embarrassed.

"I was trying to dance," he said, blushing pink.

"Only I'm not very good at it."

"Well, maybe I could teach you," said Flippy. "I'm a very good dancer. And in return, there is something that I would love you to teach me!..."

A few weeks later, Wobble, Snappy and Sparky were discussing how they missed having Flippy around, when they heard a strange and beautiful sound floating towards them through the ocean.

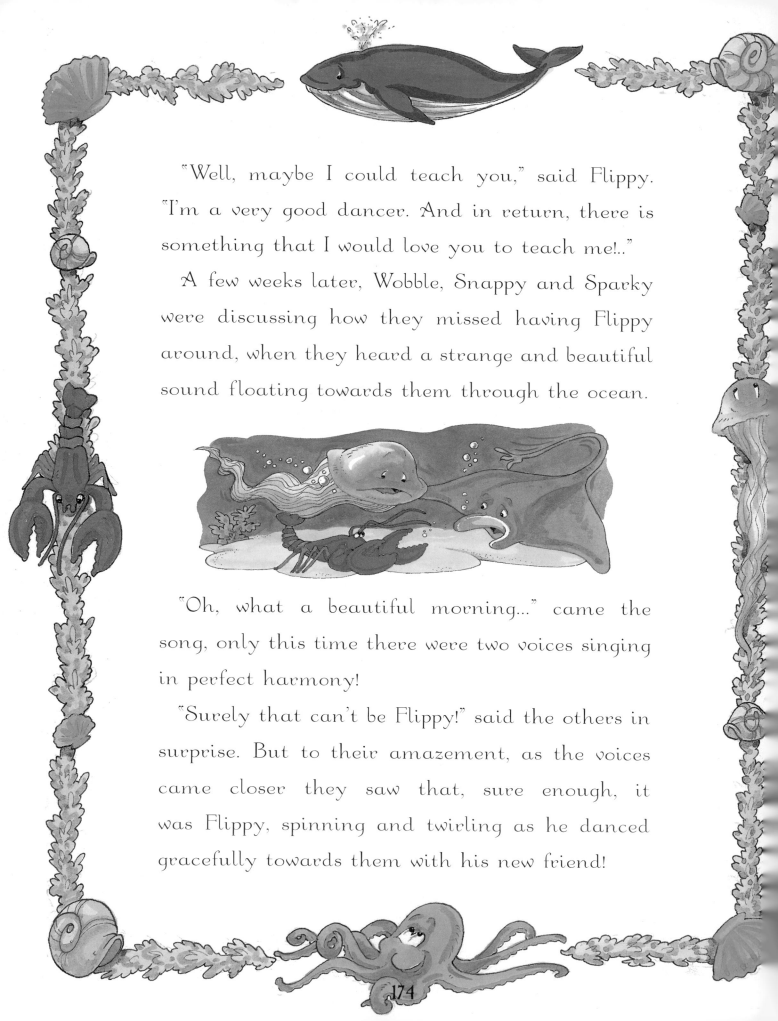

"Oh, what a beautiful morning..." came the song, only this time there were two voices singing in perfect harmony!

"Surely that can't be Flippy!" said the others in surprise. But to their amazement, as the voices came closer they saw that, sure enough, it was Flippy, spinning and twirling as he danced gracefully towards them with his new friend!

Build a House with Five Bricks

Build a house with five bricks,
One, two, three, four, five.

*Place fists on top
of each other in turn*

Make a roof

Put a roof on top,

And a chimney too,

Raise arms for chimney

Where the wind
blows through!

Blow!

176

Knock at the Door

Knock on forehead

Knock at the door,

Lift eyebrow

Peep in,

Pull ear

Ring the bell,

Push nose up

Lift the latch,

Put finger in mouth

And walk in.

Old Mother Hubbard

Old Mother Hubbard
Went to the cupboard
To fetch her poor dog a bone,
But when she got there
The cupboard was bare
And so the poor dog had none.

Tom, Tom, The Piper's Son

Tom, Tom, the piper's son,

Stole a pig and away he run!

The pig was eat, and Tom was beat,

And Tom went roaring down the street.

HAPPY HIPPOPOTAMUS

Hey! look at me,
A happy hippopotamus,
Covered with mud
From my head to my bottom-us!
Squishing and squelching
And making an awful fuss,
Rolling around in my bath!

I like to blow bubbles
Breath out through my nose-es,
To wriggle and jiggle
The mud through my toes-es,
And would you believe it
That I smell like roses,
When I come out of my bath!

To the tune of 'Oh, dear, what can the matter be?'

Cock-a-Doodle-Doo

Cock-a-doodle-doo!

My dame has lost her shoe,

My master's lost his fiddling stick,

And doesn't know what to do.

Cock-a-doodle-doo!

What is my dame to do?

Till master finds his fiddling stick,

She'll dance without her shoe.

Cock-a-doodle-doo!

My dame has found her shoe,

And master's found his fiddling stick,

Sing cock-a-doodle-doo.

This Little Piggy

This little piggy went to market,

This little piggy
stayed at home,

Wiggle...

each...

toe...

This little piggy had roast beef,

This little piggy had none,

And this little piggy cried,

All the way home.

in...

turn.

Tickle!

ALL THE WAY HOME

Come to the Window

Come to the window
My baby with me,
And look at the stars
That shine on the sea!
There are two little stars
That play bo-peep,

With two little fish
Far down in the deep;
And two little frogs
Cry neap, neap, neap;
I see a dear baby
That should be asleep.

Hush, Little Baby

Hush, little baby, don't say a word,

Pappa's gonna buy you a mockingbird.

If that mockingbird don't sing,

Pappa's gonna buy you a diamond ring.

If that diamond ring turns to brass,

Pappa's gonna buy you a looking glass.

If that looking glass gets broke,

Pappa's gonna buy you a billy goat.

If that billy goat don't pull,

Pappa's gonna buy you a cart and bull.

If that cart and bull turn over,

Pappa's gonna buy you a dog named Rover.

If that dog named Rover don't bark,

Pappa's gonna buy you a horse and cart.

If that horse and cart fall down,

You'll still be the sweetest little baby in town.

GREEDY BEAR

If there is one thing in the whole wide world that a teddy bear likes more than anything it is buns — big sticky cinnamon buns with sugary tops, and squishy middles. A teddy bear will do almost anything for a bun. But for one greedy little teddy bear called Clarence, sticky buns were to be his unsticking!

Rag Doll baked the most wonderful buns in the little toy cooker. She baked big buns and small buns, iced buns and raisin buns, cinnamon buns and poppy-seed buns, and even hot-cross buns! She shared them out amongst the toys in the playroom, and everybody loved them. But no-one loved them as much as Clarence.

"If you will give me your bun, I'll polish your boots!" he'd say to Tin Soldier.

And sometimes if Tin Soldier was not feeling too hungry, he'd agree. There was always someone who would give Clarence their bun in return for a favor, and sometimes Clarence would eat five or six buns in one day!

Then he'd be busy washing the dolls' dresses, brushing Scotty Dog's fur, or cleaning the toy policeman's car. He would even stand still and let the clown throw custard pies at him!

So you see, Clarence was not a lazy bear, but he was a greedy bear, and in spite of all his busyness, he was becoming a rather plump little greedy bear. All those buns were starting to show around his middle, and his fur was beginning to strain at the seams!

Then one day Clarence rushed into the playroom full of excitement. His owner, Penny, had told him that next week she was taking him on a teddy bears' picnic.

"She says there will be honey sandwiches and

ice-cream and cookies — and lots and lots of buns!"
Clarence told the others, rubbing his hands
together. "I can hardly wait! In fact all this
excitement has made me hungry, so I think I'll
have a bun." And he took a big sticky bun out
from under a cushion where he'd hidden it earlier.

"Oh, Clarence!" said Rabbit. "One of these days
you will simply go pop!"

"Just be happy I don't like carrots!" said
Clarence with a smile.

Well, that week Clarence was busier than ever. Every time he thought about the picnic it made him feel hungry, and then he'd have to find someone who'd let him have their bun. He ate bun after bun, and would not listen when Rag Doll warned him that his back seam was starting to come undone.

The day of the teddy bears' picnic dawned, and Clarence yawned and stretched, smiling to himself with excitement. But as he stretched he felt a strange popping sensation all down his stomach. He tried to sit up in bed, but to his alarm he found he could not move. He looked down to see that the seams around his tummy had popped open, and his stuffing was spilling out all over the bed!

"Help!" he cried. "I'm exploding!"

Just then, Penny woke up. "Oh, Clarence!" she cried when she saw him. "I can't take you to the teddy bears' picnic like that!"

Penny showed Clarence to her mommy, who said he would have to go to the toy hospital.

Clarence was away from the playroom for a whole week, but when he came back he was as good as new. Some of his stuffing had been taken out, and he was all sewn up again.

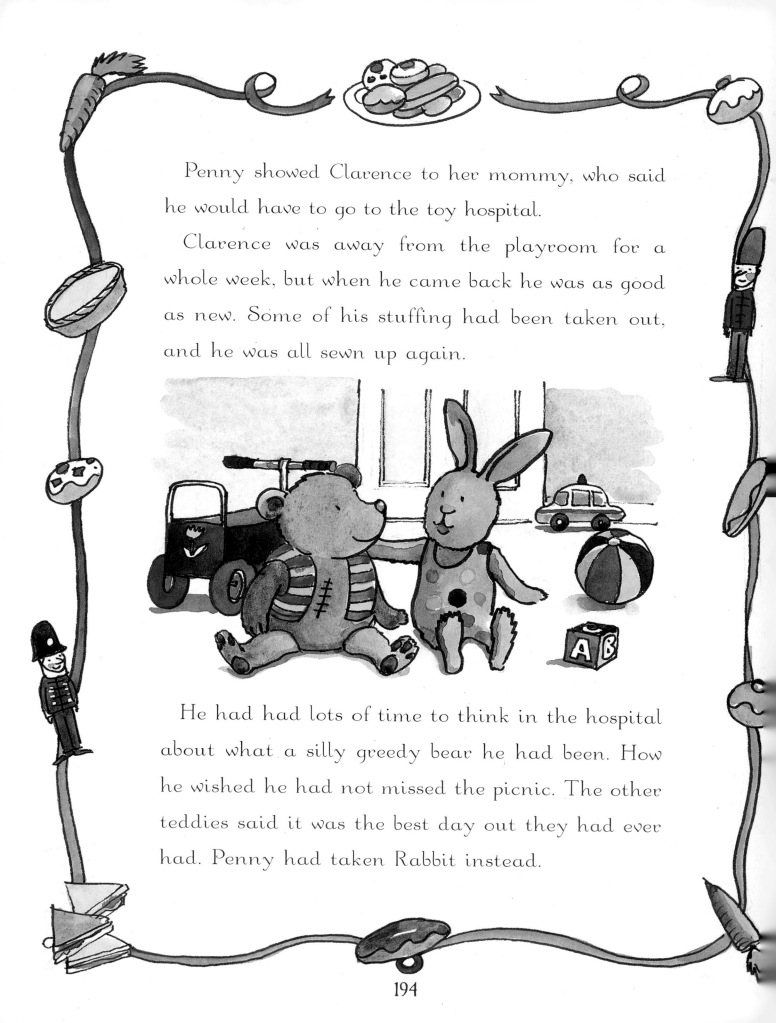

He had had lots of time to think in the hospital about what a silly greedy bear he had been. How he wished he had not missed the picnic. The other teddies said it was the best day out they had ever had. Penny had taken Rabbit instead.

"It was terrible," moaned Rabbit. "Not a carrot in sight. I did save you a bun though." And he pulled a big sticky bun out of his pocket.

"No thank you, Rabbit," said Clarence. "Funnily enough, I've gone off buns!"

Of course, Clarence did not stop eating buns for long, but from then on he stuck to one a day. And he still did favors for the others, only now he did them for free!

Ten Little Men

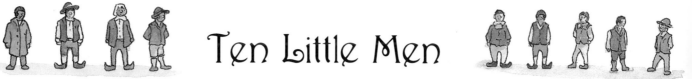

Ten little men standing straight,
Ten little men open the gate,
Ten little men all in a ring,

Hold up ten fingers

TEN LITTLE MEN...

Turn wrists

OPEN THE GATE...

Make fingers into ring

ALL IN A RING...

Ten little men bow to the king,
Ten little men dance all day,
Ten little men hide away.

Bend fingers

BOW...

Dance fingers

DANCE...

Hide hands behind back

...HIDE AWAY

Grand Old Duke of York

The grand old Duke of York,

He had ten thousand men;

He marched them up to the top of the hill;

Then he marched them down again.

And when they were up they were up.

And when they were down they were down.

And when they were only halfway up,

They were neither up nor down.

Bye, Baby Bunting

Bye, Baby Bunting
Daddy's gone a-hunting,
To find a little rabbit skin,
To wrap his Baby Bunting in.

Incy Wincy Spider

Incy Wincy Spider climbing up the spout,
Down came the rain and washed the spider out.
Out came the sun, and dried up all the rain,
Incy Wincy Spider climbed up the spout again.

Touch opposite index fingers and thumbs together by twisting wrists

CLIMBING UP THE SPOUT...

Wiggle fingers as you lower them

DOWN CAME THE RAIN...

Make a big circle with arms. Repeat first action.

OUT CAME THE SUN...

POOR LITTLE TED

Poor little Ted
Fell out of bed,
And found that he had
A big bump on his head!

He let out a scream,
I woke from my dream,
And soon made him better
With cake and ice-cream!

IN A SPIN

I had a little teddy,
He went everywhere with me,
But now I've gone and lost him,
Oh, where can my teddy be?

I've looked behind the sofa,
I've looked beneath the bed,
I've looked out in the garden,
And in the garden shed!

I've looked inside the bathtub,
And underneath my chair,
Oh, where, oh, where is Teddy?
I've hunted everywhere!

At last I try the kitchen,
My face breaks in a grin.
There's Teddy in the washtub –
Mom's sent him for a spin!

London Bridge Is Falling Down

London bridge is falling down,
Falling down, falling down,
London bridge is falling down,
My fair lady.

Build it up with wood and clay,
Wood and clay, wood and clay,
Build it up with wood and clay,
My fair lady

Wood and clay will wash away,
Wash away, wash away,
Wood and clay will wash away,
My fair lady.

Build it up with bricks and mortar,
Bricks and mortar, bricks and mortar,
Build it up with bricks and mortar,
My fair lady.

Bricks and mortar will not stay,
Will not stay, will not stay,
Bricks and mortar will not stay,
My fair lady.

Build it up with iron and steel,
Iron and steel, iron and steel,
Build it up with iron and steel,
My fair lady.

Iron and steel will bend and bow,
Bend and bow, bend and bow
Iron and steel will bend and bow,
My fair lady.

Build it up with silver and gold,
Silver and gold, silver and gold,
Build it up with silver and gold,
My fair lady.

Silver and gold will be stolen away,
Stolen away, stolen away,
Silver and gold will be stolen away,
My fair lady.

Set a man to watch all night,
Watch all night, watch all night,
Set a man to watch all night,
My fair lady.

There Was a Little Turtle

There was a little turtle,
He lived in a box.
He swam in a puddle,
He climbed on the rocks.

He snapped at a mosquito,
He snapped at a flea.
He snapped at a minnow,
He snapped at me.

Cup both palms, one on top of the other

...LITTLE TURTLE

Draw a square in the air with index fingers

...IN A BOX

Making swimming motion with hand

...SWAM IN A PUDDLE

Waggle all five fingers in crawling motion

...ON THE ROCKS

He caught the mosquito,
He caught the flea.
He caught the minnow,

But... he didn't catch me!

Snap thumb and fingers together four times

Clap hands together three times

Shake head and point to chin

HE SNAPPED...

HE CAUGHT...

...DIDN'T CATCH ME!

THE COW WHO JUMPED OVER THE MOON

Boing, boing, boing! Bouncy Bunny kicked up her heels and bounded across the field.

"I can bounce high in the air, watch me!" she called to the other animals on the farm. Her fluffy white tail bobbed up and down.

"Very good!" said Silly Sheep, who was easily impressed.

"Yes, very good," said Swift, the sheepdog. "But not as good as me. I can jump right over the gate."

With that, he leapt over the gate and into the field.

"Amazing!" said Silly Sheep.

"Yes, amazing," said Harry Horse, with a flick of his mane. "But not as amazing as me. I can jump right over that hedge. Watch me!" And with that, he galloped around the field, then leapt high into the air, and sailed over the tall hedge.

"Unbelievable!" said Silly Sheep.

"Yes, unbelievable," said Daisy, the cow, chewing lazily on a clump of grass. "But not as unbelievable as me. I can jump right over the moon!"

"Well, I'm afraid that is unbelievable, Daisy," said Harry Horse. "No one can jump over the moon. That's just a fairy story."

"Well, I can," said Daisy, stubbornly. "And I can prove it! You can watch me do it if you like!"

The other animals all agreed that they would very much like to see Daisy jump over the moon.

"Meet me here in the field tonight, then," said Daisy to them. "When the moon is full, and the stars are shining bright."

So that night, when the moon had risen high up in the sky, the excited animals gathered together in the field. The rest of the animals from the farm came along too, for word had soon spread that Daisy the cow was going to jump over the moon, and they were all eager to watch.

"Come along then, Daisy," said Swift, the sheepdog, as the animals waited impatiently. "Are you going to show us how you can jump over the moon, or not?"

All the animals laughed, as they thought that Daisy was just boasting, and that she would not really be able to do it.

"Yes, I am going to show you," said Daisy, "but first of all, you will have to come with me. This isn't the right spot." Daisy led the animals across the field, to the far side, where a little stream ran along the edge of the field, separating it from the dark woods on the other side.

"Now, stand back everyone, and give me some room," said Daisy. The animals did as they were asked, and watched Daisy with anticipation, giggling nervously. Whatever was she going to do?

Daisy trotted back to the middle of the field, then ran towards the stream at a great speed.

At the last moment, she sprang into the air, and sailed across the stream, landing safely on the other side.

"I did it!" cried Daisy. "Aren't you going to clap, then?" The other animals looked at each other in confusion.

"But you only jumped over the stream!" said Harry Horse, puzzled.

"Come and take a closer look," called Daisy, still on the far side. The animals gathered close to the water's edge. They looked down, and there reflected in the water shimmered the great full moon! How the animals laughed when they realised Daisy had tricked them.

"See?" said Daisy. "I really can jump over the moon!" And just to prove it, she jumped back to the field again. The animals all clapped and cheered.

"That was a very good trick!" said Swift.

"Amazing!" said Silly Sheep. "Could someone explain it to me again, please!.."

Two Little Men in a Flying Saucer

Move arms up and down

Two little men in a flying saucer
Flew round the world one day.

Lift baby in circle

They looked to the left and right a bit,
And couldn't bear the sight of it,

Turn head left

Turn head right

Cover eyes

Repeat first action

Tall Shop

Raise arms above head

Tall shop in the town.

Move hands up and down

Lifts moving up and down.

Swing forearms open and shut

Doors swinging round about.

Move fists back and forth

People moving in and out.

Tommy Thumb

Tommy Thumb,
Tommy Thumb,
Where are you?
Here I am, here I am,
How do you do?

Peter pointer, etc,
Middle Man, etc.
Ruby Ring, etc.
Baby Small, etc.

*Make fists, raise thumbs
and wiggle them*

TOMMY THUMB...

*Raise forefingers and
wiggle them*

PETER POINTER...

*Raise middle fingers and
wiggle them*

MIDDLE MAN...

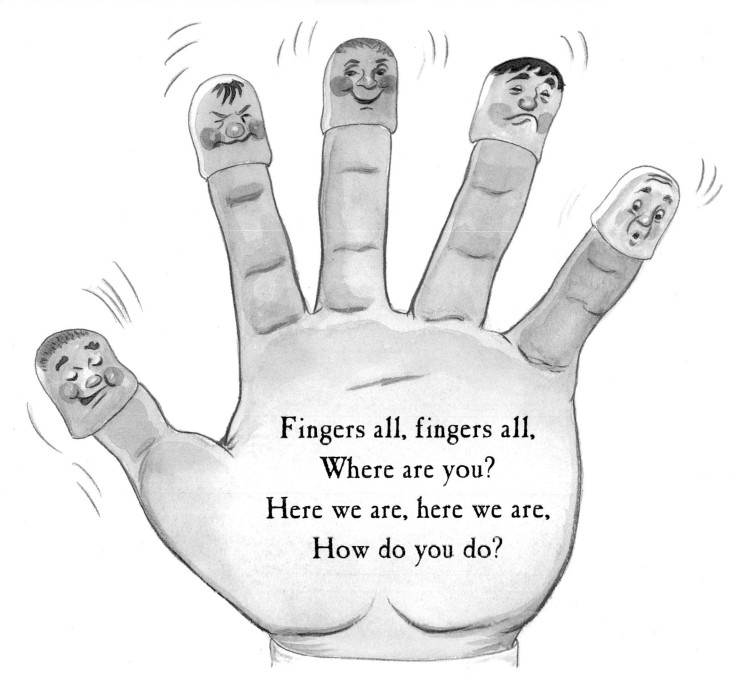

Fingers all, fingers all,
Where are you?
Here we are, here we are,
How do you do?

Raise ring fingers and wiggle them

RUBY RING...

Raise little fingers and wiggle them

BABY SMALL...

Raise ALL fingers and wiggle them

FINGERS ALL...

The Muffin Man

Have you seen the muffin man,
The muffin man, the muffin man?
Have you seen the muffin man,
He lives in Drury Lane?
Oh yes, I've seen the muffin man,
The muffin man, the muffin man.
Oh yes, I've seen the muffin man,
He lives in Drury Lane.

Old King Cole

Old King Cole was a merry old soul,
And a merry old soul was he;
He called for his pipe,
And he called for his bowl,
And he called for his fiddlers three.

TEA WITH THE QUEEN

Teddy bear, teddy bear,
Where have you been?
I've been up to London to visit the queen!

I went to her palace,
And knocked at the gate,
And one of her soldiers said, please would I wait?

Then one of her footmen,
All dressed in red,
Led me inside, saying, step this way, Ted!

And there in a huge room,
High on her throne,
Sat the poor queen, taking tea all alone.

She said, how delightful,
Sit down, fill your tum!
And soon we were chattering just like old chums!

And when time came to leave,
She shook hands and then,
She said, come back soon, we must do it again!

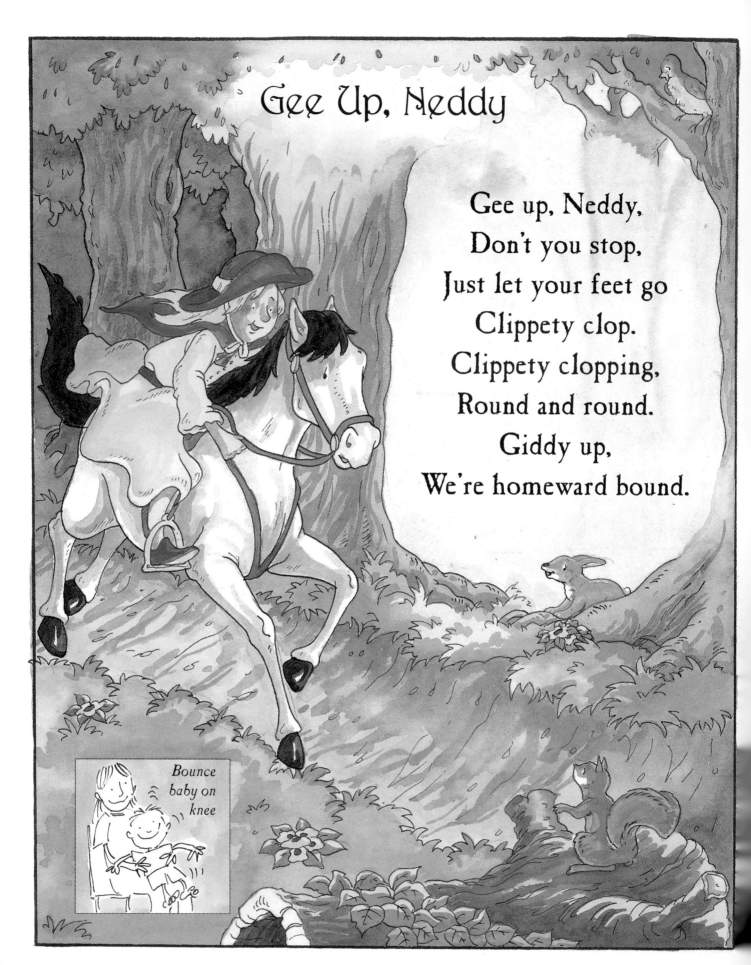

Gee Up, Neddy

Gee up, Neddy,
Don't you stop,
Just let your feet go
Clippety clop.
Clippety clopping,
Round and round.
Giddy up,
We're homeward bound.

Bounce baby on knee

226

Hickory Dickory Dock

Walk fingers up arm

Clap once

Walk fingers down arm

Hickory
dickory dock,
The mouse ran
up the clock.

The clock
struck one,

The mouse
ran down,
Hickory
dickory dock.

THE SNOW BEARS

Jerry and Humphrey were two teddy bears who had been friends for as long as they could remember. They lived with a little girl called Millie, who kept them on her bed. From the top of her pillows they could see outside through the window, and they loved to look at the garden as it changed through the seasons.

One cold winter's morning, Millie jumped out of bed, flung open the curtains and let out a squeal of delight. "Snow!"

She rushed over to her closet and began to pull on some clothes. Jerry and Humphrey watched in amazement as she put on a t-shirt, pants, socks, a shirt, two sweaters, a vest, a hat, a scarf, mittens and last of all her coat! What a lot of clothes!

"It's going to be cold out there," she explained to the little bears. "Much too cold for you two! Watch me, I'm going to build a snowman!" And with that, she ran downstairs and out into the yard.

"Too cold!" said Humphrey, with a sniff, when she'd gone. "What does she mean, too cold? We're bears! We like the cold!"

"Besides, our furry coats would keep us warm," said Jerry. "By the way, what's a snowman?"

"I don't know," said Humphrey. "Let's watch through the window and see if we can find out."

The little bears looked on as Millie ran and jumped and leapt about in the snow.

It was so deep that it almost came to the top of her rubber boots. Millie laughed and shrieked with delight as she threw snowballs at the old oak tree, and slid down a little slope at the end of the yard on her sled.

"That looks like fun!" said Jerry. "I wish we were out there too!"

"So do I," said Humphrey, glumly. "It's far too stuffy in this warm house. A good dose of chilly air is just what a bear needs now and then to clear out the cobwebs!"

The little bears turned back to the window, and watched intently, as Millie gathered lots of snow together, and built it into a big ball, with a smaller ball on top. She fixed stones in place for eyes and a mouth, and took a carrot out of her coat pocket which she stuck in place of a nose. Then she put a scarf and hat on her snowy statue, and stood back to admire her work with her hands on her hips, smiling proudly.

"That must be a snowman!" said Humphrey.

"We could make one of those," said Jerry, with a twinkle in his eye. Humphrey and Jerry looked at each other, and smiled a secret smile.

That night, when they were sure that Millie was fast asleep, Humphrey and Jerry opened the window carefully, so as not to wake her, slid down the drainpipe into the yard, and smiled as they felt the chilly snow beneath their paws.

The trees sparkled in the moonlight as large snowflakes softly floated down and settled all around. Soon the two teddy bear friends were having a wonderful time chasing each other and running and tumbling through the snow.

They laughed and played until the first rays of sun peeked through the trees, then they quickly clambered up the drainpipe and back inside to bed. They lay whispering and giggling together with excitement, as they chuckled at the great adventure they had had.

The next morning, when Millie threw open the curtains, she was delighted to see the yard still thickly covered with snow. But imagine her surprise when she looked at the snowman she had built and saw two snowbears sitting beside him!

"How on earth?.." she muttered, scratching her head in bewilderment. Then she spotted a trail of watery paw prints leading from the window, across the floor to the bed, where the two little bears lay watching her.

"What have you two been up to?" she asked. But the little bears just smiled a secret smile.

"Come on," cried Millie, scooping them up. "We're going to play outside!

There Was an Old Woman

There was an old woman
Who lived in a shoe,
She had so many children
She didn't know what to do.
She gave them some broth
Without any bread,
And kissed them all soundly
And sent them to bed.

One, Two, Buckle My Shoe

One, two, buckle my shoe,
Three, four, knock at the door;
Five, six, pick up sticks,
Seven, eight, lay them straight;
Nine, ten, a good fat hen,
Eleven, twelve, dig and delve;
Thirteen, fourteen, maids a-courting,
Fifteen, sixteen, maids in the kitchen;
Seventeen, eighteen, maids a-waiting,
Nineteen, twenty, my plate's empty.

See-Saw, Margery Daw

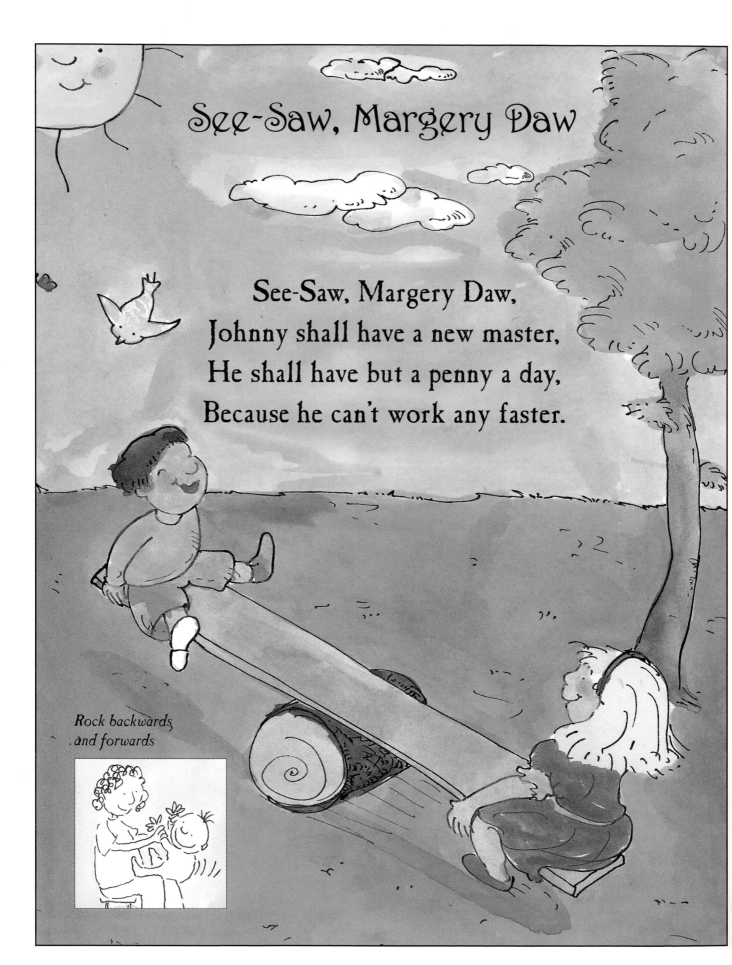

See-Saw, Margery Daw,
Johnny shall have a new master,
He shall have but a penny a day,
Because he can't work any faster.

Rock backwards
and forwards

Here is the Church

Here is the church,

Here is the steeple,

Interlace fingers

Point index fingers

Open the doors,

And here are the people.

Open thumbs

Turn hands over and wiggle fingers

Here is the parson, going upstairs,

And here he is a-saying his prayers.

Walk fingers of one hand up fingers of other hand

Place palms together

The Owl and the Pussy-cat

The Owl and the Pussy-cat went to sea

In a beautiful pea-green boat,

They took some honey, and plenty of money,

Wrapped up in a five-pound note.

The Owl looked up to the stars above,

And sang to a small guitar,

"O lovely Pussy! O Pussy, my love,

What a beautiful Pussy you are,

You are, you are!

What a beautiful Pussy you are!"

Pussy said to the Owl, "You elegant fowl!

How charmingly sweet you sing!

"O let us be married! Too long we have tarried:

But what shall we do for a ring?"

They sailed away, for a year and a day,

To the land where the Bong-tree grows,

And there in a wood a Piggy-wig stood,

With a ring at the end of his nose,

His nose, his nose,

With a ring at the end of his nose.

"Dear Pig, are you willing to sell for one shilling
Your ring?" Said the Piggy, "I will."
So they took it away, and were married next day
By the Turkey who lives on the hill.

They dined on mince, and slices of quince,
Which they ate with a runcible spoon;
And hand in hand, on the edge of the sand,
They danced by the light of the moon,
The moon, the moon,
They danced by the light of the moon.

Lucy Locket

Lucy Locket lost her pocket,
Kitty Fisher found it.
Not a penny was there in it,
Only ribbon round it.

Cinderella's umbrella's
Full of holes all over.
Every time it starts to rain
She has to run for cover.

Aladdin's lamp is getting damp,
And is no longer gleaming.
It doesn't spark within the dark,
But you can't stop it steaming.

Turn Around

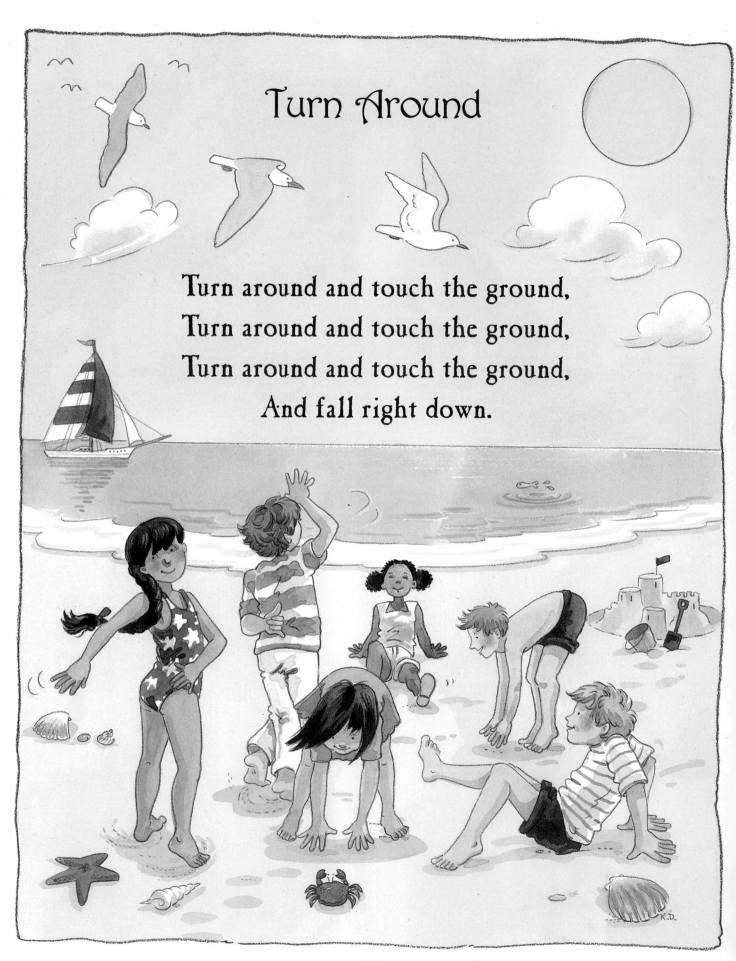

Turn around and touch the ground,
Turn around and touch the ground,
Turn around and touch the ground,
And fall right down.

The Baby in the Cradle

The baby in the cradle
Goes rock-a-rock-a-rock.

The clock on the dresser
Goes tick-a-tick-a-tock.

The rain on the window
Goes tap-a-tap-a-tap,

But here comes the sun,
So we clap-a-clap-a-clap!

Rock arms

ROCK

Swing arm side to side

TICK-TOCK

Tap finger on hand

TAP-A-TAP

Clap!

CLAP

BEARS AHOY

One summer's day, three little boys went for a picnic by the bank of a river. They took with them their swimming things, some cheese and tomato sandwiches and, of course, their teddy bears.

When they arrived, they found a small boat tied to a tree. The boys climbed on board, taking their teddies with them, and had a great game of pirates. The boys pretended to walk the plank, and soon they were all splashing about, playing and swimming in the river. They chased each other through the shallow water, and disappeared along the river and out of sight.

Now, the three bears left on board the boat did
not get on very well together. Oscar was a small,
honey-colored bear. He was good friends with
Mabel, who had shaggy brown fur, but neither of
them liked Toby. He was bigger than they were
and he was a bully. He was always growling at
the other bears and telling them what to do.

As soon as the boys were out of sight, Toby
leapt to his feet. The boat rocked. Oscar and
Mabel begged him to sit down.

"I'm a fearless sailor," cried Toby. "I've sailed the seven seas and now I'm going to sail them again." He untied the boat, and pushed it away from the bank. The boat lurched from side to side.

"Come on, crew. Look lively!" shouted Toby. "Do as I say or I'll make you walk the plank." Now that it was untied, the little blue boat began to drift. It turned sideways gently, then caught the main current and began to gather speed.

"Toby!" cried Oscar. "We're moving!"

"Of course we are, you big softie," growled Toby. "We're bold and fearless pirates on the high seas."

Oscar and Mabel clung together in fright, as the little boat sailed down the river, past fields and houses. "Help!" they shouted. "Toby, make it stop!" But Toby was having a great time.

"Ha, ha," shouted Toby. "This is the life!"

Oscar glanced over the side. He wished he hadn't. The sight of everything passing by so quickly made him feel seasick.

"Look out, Toby!" he cried. "We're going to hit the bank. Steer it away."

But Toby did nothing. The boat hit the bank with a thump and Toby fell forward. The boat swung round and headed for the middle of the river once more.

"Toby!" shouted Mabel. "Save us!"

But Toby was sitting in the bottom of the boat, rubbing a big bump on his head.

"I can't. I don't know how to sail a boat," he whimpered, feebly. He hid his face in his paws and began to cry. The boat zig-zagged on down the river, with the little bears clinging on to the sides in fright. In time, the river became wider and they could hear the cry of seagulls.

"Oh, Toby," cried Mabel. "We're heading for the sea. Do something!"

"Nobody likes me," wailed Toby. "Now we're going to sink to the bottom of the sea, and you won't like me either!"

Oscar wasn't listening. He had found a rope hanging from the sail. "Let's put the sail up and see if it will blow us to shore," he said.

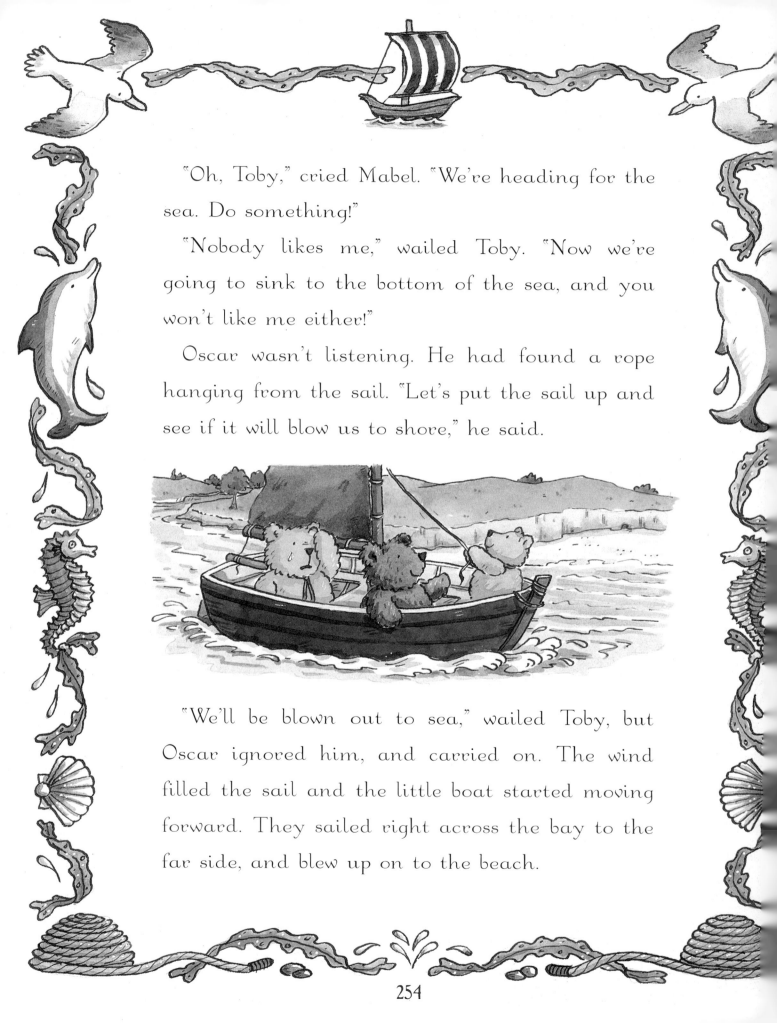

"We'll be blown out to sea," wailed Toby, but Oscar ignored him, and carried on. The wind filled the sail and the little boat started moving forward. They sailed right across the bay to the far side, and blew up on to the beach.

"Oh, Oscar, you are a hero!" sighed Mabel, hugging him tight. "You saved us!"

Imagine the bears' surprise to see the three little boys running towards them along the beach — they had gone to find the coastguard and raise the alarm. There were hugs and kisses all round when they found the bears safe and sound. And you can be sure that from that day on, Toby was a much wiser and kinder bear, and he never bullied the others again.

My Hands

My hands upon my head I place,
On my shoulders, on my face;
On my hips I place them so,
Then bend down to touch my toe.

Place hands on head

...on shoulders

...on face

...on hips

Now I raise them up so high,
Make my fingers fairly fly,
Now I clap them, one, two, three.
Then I fold them silently.

Touch toes

Raise hands in the air

Clap hands three times

Fold arms

It's Raining, It's Pouring

It's raining, it's pouring,
The old man is snoring.
He went to bed,
And bumped his head,
And couldn't get up
in the morning.

Lavender's Blue

Lavender's blue, dilly, dilly, lavender's green,

When I am king, dilly, dilly, you shall be queen;

Call up your men, dilly dilly, set them to work,

Some to the plough, dilly dilly, some to the cart;

Some to make hay, dilly, dilly, some to thresh corn;

Whilst you and I, dilly, dilly, keep ourselves warm.

The Farmer's in his Den

The farmer's in his den,
The farmer's in his den,
E I E I
The farmer's in his den.

The farmer wants a wife,
The farmer wants a wife,
E I E I
The farmer wants a wife.

The wife wants a child,
The wife wants a child,
E I E I
The wife wants a child.

The child wants a nurse,
The child wants a nurse,
E I E I
The child wants a nurse.

The nurse wants a dog,
The nurse wants a dog,
E I E I
The nurse wants a dog.

We all pat the dog,
We all pat the dog,
E I E I
We all pat the dog.

Clap, Clap Hands

Clap, clap hands, one, two, three,
Put your hands upon your knees,
Lift them up high to touch the sky,
Clap, clap hands and away they fly.

Clap hands in rhythm   *Touch knees*   *Raise arms*   *Shake raised hands*

CLAP, CLAP HANDS   ...YOUR KNEES   ...LIFT THEM HIGH   ...AWAY THEY FLY

Five Little Monkeys

Five little monkeys jumping on the bed,
One fell off and bumped his head,
Mummy phoned the doctor and the doctor said,
"No more monkeys jumping on the bed!"

Four little monkeys...
Three little monkeys...
Two little monkeys...
One little monkey...

Repeat actions showing one less finger each time

Hold up hand

FIVE LITTLE MONKEYS

Pat top of head

...BUMPED HIS HEAD

Pretend to hold phone

...PHONED THE DOCTOR

Waggle index finger

NO MORE MONKEYS...

Old MacDonald

Old MacDonald had a farm,

E...I...E...I...O

And on that farm he had some cows,

E...I...E...I...O

With a moo-moo here,

And a moo-moo there,

Here a moo, there a moo,

Everywhere a moo-moo,

Old MacDonald had a farm,

E...I...E...I...O

Old MacDonald had a farm,

E...I...E...I...O

And on that farm he had some ducks,

E...I...E...I...O

With a quack-quack here,

And a quack-quack there, *etc.*

This rhyme can be continued with other verses: sheep, baa-baa; dogs, woof-woof; horses, neigh-neigh; cats, miaow-miaow; etc. The speed can be adjusted to suit the age of the child. Older children can memorise the previous verses and add them to the rhyme, eg. 'with a quack-quack here, and a quack-quack there, here a quack, there a quack, everywhere a quack, quack, moo-moo here, moo-moo there,' etc.

These Are Grandma's Glasses

These are Grandma's glasses,
This is Grandma's hat;
Grandma claps her hands like this,
And rests them in her lap.

Make rings round eyes

Mime hat with hands

Clap hands

Place hands in lap

These are Grandpa's glasses,
This is Grandpa's hat;
Grandpa folds his arms like this,
And has a little nap.

Make rings round eyes

Mime hat with hands

Fold arms

Pretend to sleep

Mousie

*Make a fist and push
other index finger in*

MOUSIE CREEPING

*Push finger through
until end appears*

MOUSIE PEEPING

Wiggle finger

I'D LIKE TO STAY...

*Pull finger back
suddenly and hide!*

...POPS INTO HOLE

Mousie comes a-creeping, creeping.
Mousie comes a-peeping, peeping.
Mousie says, "I'd like to stay,
But I haven't time today."
Mousie pops into his hole
And says, "ACHOO!
I've caught a cold!"

267

LAZY LION

Lazy Lion lay snoozing in the shade of a tree. The hot sun beat down, as he lazily flicked at the buzzing flies with his tail.

There was nothing Lazy Lion liked to do more than sleep. He would sleep all night and all day if he could, just waking up every once in a while to have a snack.

"Hmm," he purred to himself. "This is the life. Nothing to do all day but lie in the sun and sleep. Perfect!"

Just then, a laughing hyena came running by.

"Wake up, Lazy Lion!" he chuckled. "Unless you feel like going for a swim!? Rain's coming!"

Lazy Lion opened one eye. "Silly creature!" he said with a sniff, as he watched the hyena running far off into the distance, still laughing. "He's just trying to trick me into waking up and moving!" and he closed his eyes and went back to sleep.

A short while later someone nudged his behind.

"Wake up, Lazy Lion. Rain's coming." Giraffe was bending her long neck down and nudging him with her nose. "You should head for shelter. The river might flood!"

"Don't be ridiculous!" said Lion. "Hyena's been filling your head with his nonsense, I see!" and he closed his eyes and was snoring again in seconds.

But he had not been dozing for long when he felt something tugging at his whiskers.

"Wake up, Lazy Lion!" It was a little mouse.

"Rain's coming. Could you please carry my children and I to safety?" asked the mouse.

"Oh, I'm far too busy for that," said Lazy Lion. "Besides, what's all this talk of rain? It's a fine, sunny day!" And with that, he closed his eyes and went back to sleep.

A few moments later he was woken by something pulling at his tail. It was Monkey.

"Wake up, Lazy Lion. Rain's coming. Could you help carry my bananas up to the rocks?"

"Why does everyone keep waking me?" asked Lazy Lion, crossly. "Can't you see I'm busy?"

"Sorry, Lion, but you didn't look busy to me," said Monkey.

"Well, I am!" growled Lion. "I'm very busy thinking what to do with the next person who wakes me up!" And he gave Monkey a mean stare, before shutting his eyes tight once more.

After that, none of the animals dared to wake Lazy Lion up again. So they couldn't warn him that the dark storm clouds were gathering, and the first drops of rain had started to fall.

They just hurried high up to the safety of the rocks and caves and took shelter from the storm that was on its way.

Lazy Lion gave a little shiver, as he lay dreaming. A big raindrop fell on his nose. Then another, and another. Lion stirred. "Oh, bother," he thought to himself. "It's raining. Well, it's probably only a light shower. I'll snooze a little longer." He settled back down to sleep.

But the rain began to fall harder, and harder. Soon Lazy Lion's thick fur was wet through, and he was starting to feel cold and uncomfortable. But he was still too lazy to get up and move to the shelter of the rocks. "I'll just sleep for five more minutes!" he told himself.

But as the minutes passed the rain fell harder and harder, and the river rose higher and higher. Then, with a huge crash of thunder, and a bright flash of lightening, the river broke its banks and came flooding across the plains! All of a sudden, Lazy Lion found himself being tossed around as he struggled to keep his head above the stormy waters.

The other animals watched in horror from the safety of the rocks as Lazy Lion was dragged below the water by the strong current.

Then suddenly his big strong head popped up again, and he gasped for breath.

Lazy Lion swam with all his might towards the rocks, as the other animals cheered him on.

"Oh, this is hard work!" he panted. How he wished he had listened to the others and had not been so lazy.

At last he made it, and he struggled up onto the rocks, wet through and worn out. The other animals gathered round, anxiously.

"Are you all right, Lazy Lion?" asked Monkey.

"I'm exhausted!" panted Lazy Lion, then added, "But it's nothing a good sleep won't cure!"

I Saw a Slippery, Slithery Snake

I saw a slippery, slithery snake
Slide through the grasses,
Making them shake.

Weave hands side to side

Circle eyes

He looked at me with his
beady eye.

Go away!

"Go away from my pretty
green garden," said I.

Repeat first action

"**Sssss**," said the
slippery, slithery snake,
As he slid through the grasses,
Making them shake.

Foxy's Hole

Put your finger in
Foxy's hole.
Foxy's not at home.
Foxy's out at the
back door
A-picking at a bone.

*Interlock fingers leaving a hole
between middle and ring finger*

... FINGER IN FOXY'S HOLE

Get child to put finger in hole

FOXY'S NOT AT HOME

Nip child's finger with thumbs

A-PICKING AT A BONE

Pussy Cat, Pussy Cat

Pussy cat, pussy cat, where have you been?

I've been up to London to visit the Queen.

Pussy cat, pussy cat, what did you there?

I frightened a little mouse under her chair.

Diddle, Diddle, Dumpling

Diddle, diddle, dumpling, my son John,

Went to bed with his trousers on;

One shoe off, one shoe on,

Diddle, diddle, dumpling, my son John.

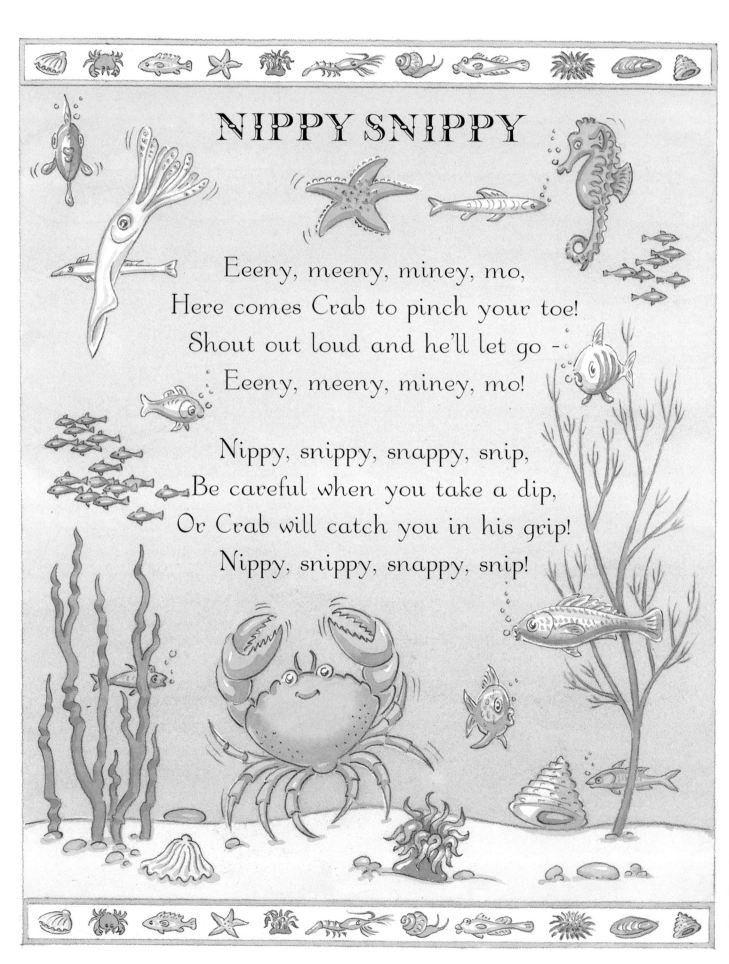

NIPPY SNIPPY

Eeeny, meeny, miney, mo,
Here comes Crab to pinch your toe!
Shout out loud and he'll let go -
Eeeny, meeny, miney, mo!

Nippy, snippy, snappy, snip,
Be careful when you take a dip,
Or Crab will catch you in his grip!
Nippy, snippy, snappy, snip!

ACHOO!

Mouse's eyes filled up with water,
His little nose started to twitch,
A tingling tickled his whiskers,
And then his knees started to itch.

He got a bad case of the hiccups,
Then threw back his head in a sneeze,
And he said, "I'm most awfully sorry,
It's just I'm allergic to cheese!"

Ring-A-Ring O'Roses

Ring-a-ring o'roses,
A pocket full of posies,
A-tishoo! A-tishoo!
We all fall down!

Dance around in a ring, pretend to sneeze, then fall down on the floor

Pop Goes the Weasel

Half a pound of tu'penny rice,
Half a pound of treacle.
That's the way the money goes,
POP! Goes the weasel.

A bouncing on the knee rhyme, with an extra big bounce on the "Pop!"

Lazy Mary

Lazy Mary will you get up,

Will you get up, will you get up?

Lazy Mary will you get up,

Will you get up today?

Six o'clock and you're still sleeping,

Daylight's creeping o'er your windowsill.

Lazy Mary will you get up,

Will you get up, will you get up?

Lazy Mary will you get up,

Will you get up today?

Seven o'clock and you're still snoring,
Sunshine's pouring through your window pane.

Lazy Mary will you get up,
Will you get up, will you get up?
Lazy Mary will you get up,
Will you get up today?

Eight o'clock, you've missed your train,
Can you explain why you're still in your bed?

Girls and Boys

Girls and boys come out to play,

The moon doth shine as bright as day,

Leave your supper and leave your sleep,

And come with your playfellows into the street.

Come with a whoop, come with a call,

Come with a good will, or come not at all.

Up the ladder and down the wall,

A halfpenny bun will serve us all.

You find milk and I'll find flour,

And we'll have pudding in half an hour.

Jello on the Plate

Jello on the plate,
Jello on the plate,
Wibble, wobble,
Wibble, wobble,
Jello on the plate.

Rock from side to side

Bounce up and down

Candies in the jar,
Candies in the jar,
Shake them up,
Shake them up,
Candies in the jar.

Candles on the cake,
Candles on the cake,
Blow them out,
Blow them out,
Puff, PUFF, **PUFF!**

Blow!

290

Here's the Lady's Knives and Forks

Here's the lady's knives and forks.
Here's the lady's table.
Here's the lady's looking glass.
And here's the baby's cradle.
Rock! Rock! Rock! Rock!

Interlock fingers with backs of hands together

KNIVES AND FORKS...

Turn hands over and bring wrists together

TABLE...

Raise both index fingers

LOOKING GLASS...

Raise both little fingers and rock back and forth

CRADLE - ROCK!

TOUGH TED
LOSES HIS GROWL

The alarm clock started to ring and Katie jumped out of bed, bursting with energy. Tough Ted opened one sleepy eye (which was all he could do, as the other one had fallen off years ago) and stretched.

"Another morning," he yawned. "I don't suppose it will be a good one."

Tough Ted was a very old bear. He had belonged to Katie's mom when she was young. He had been a smart teddy then, and happy, but now he was in a sorry state and was always grumpy. He was the oldest of the toys and he had been through some tough times. The other toys loved him, but they were fed up with his constant moaning and groaning.

"When is this bed going to be made? I can't get comfortable with all these covers thrown back!" he complained. "And they should pull that blind down, the sun's shining straight into my eye," he grumbled.

293

"Talking of which, it's about time they gave me a new one," he moaned. He carried on growling all morning.

"If he doesn't stop complaining soon I'm going to stuff my hat in his mouth," whispered Soldier to Clown, as they sat on the shelf.

"Not if I put my juggling balls in there first!" said Clown. All the toys giggled.

"It's about time we taught him a lesson," said Rag Doll. "What can we do to stop him moaning?"

"What about sticking a band-aid over his mouth while he's asleep?" twittered Owl, who was always wise.

"That's a brilliant idea, Owl!" said Rag Doll, and everyone agreed.

So that night, Rag Doll fetched a band-aid from the bathroom cabinet, and stuck it firmly over Tough Ted's mouth while he was asleep. All the toys were delighted – peace and quiet at last!

The next morning the alarm went off and Katie went into the bathroom. Tough Ted opened his eye and was just about to moan that the alarm was still ringing, when he realized he could not open his mouth!

He pulled and stretched and twisted his face as hard as he could, but he could not get his mouth to open. Then he noticed that all the toys were watching him. When he looked and saw the band-aid in the mirror he was furious! He ripped it off and turned to face the other toys angrily.

"Who did this?" he bellowed. "When I find out who it was, there'll be trouble, growwwll! Have you no respect for an old bear?" He went on and on and on. He grew red in the face, and looked terribly cross. All the toys became quite scared.

Then, as he was growling at the top of his voice, a funny thing happened. His voice began to crack. He tried to clear his throat, but it was no use. He had lost his voice completely!

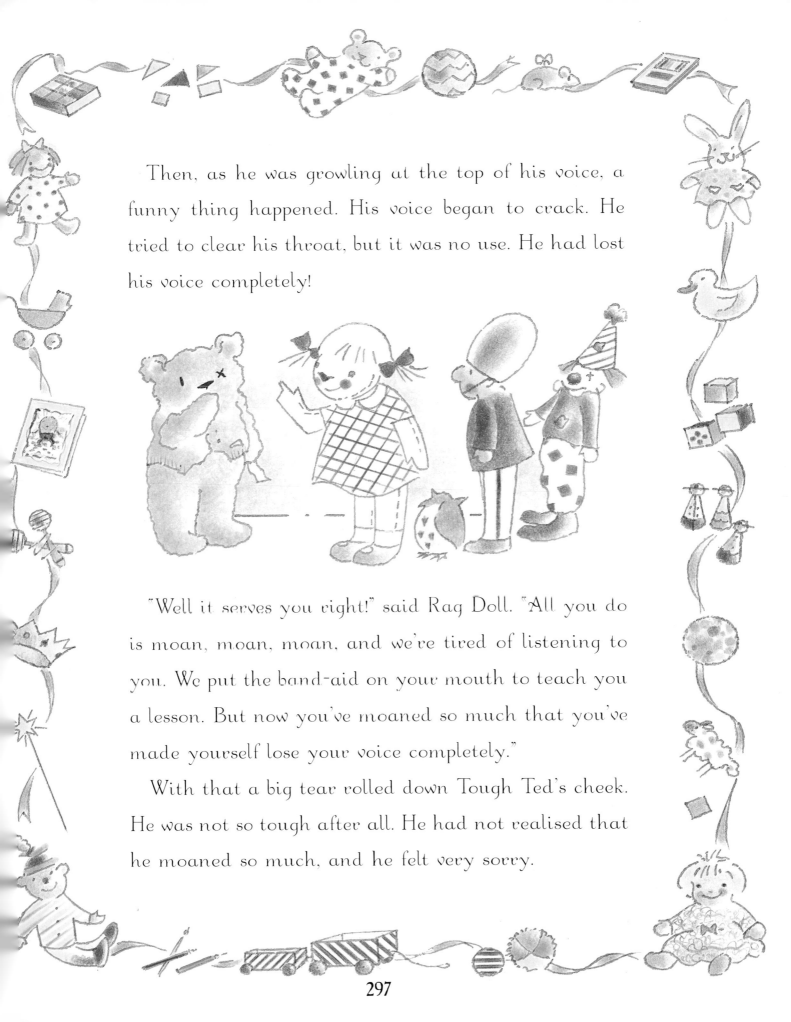

"Well it serves you right!" said Rag Doll. "All you do is moan, moan, moan, and we're tired of listening to you. We put the band-aid on your mouth to teach you a lesson. But now you've moaned so much that you've made yourself lose your voice completely."

With that a big tear rolled down Tough Ted's cheek. He was not so tough after all. He had not realised that he moaned so much, and he felt very sorry.

Rag Doll did not like seeing Tough Ted so sad. All the toys felt a bit guilty for what they had done.

"I'll go and get you some honey from the kitchen," said Rag Doll. "It will soothe your throat. But you must promise not to start moaning again."

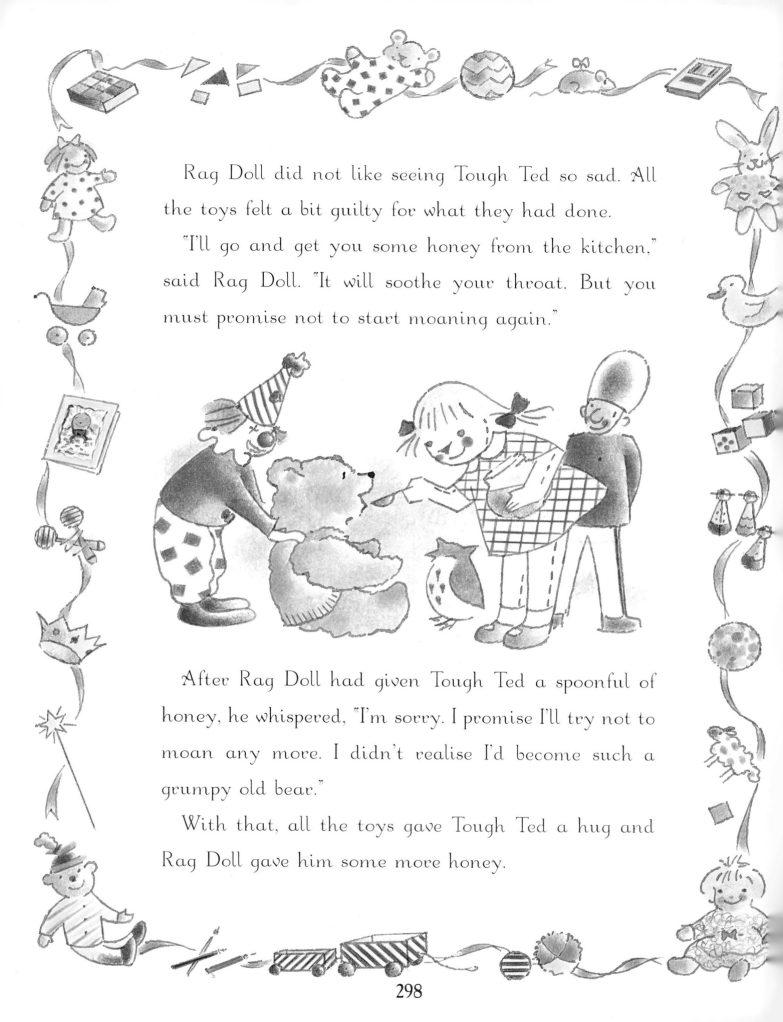

After Rag Doll had given Tough Ted a spoonful of honey, he whispered, "I'm sorry. I promise I'll try not to moan any more. I didn't realise I'd become such a grumpy old bear."

With that, all the toys gave Tough Ted a hug and Rag Doll gave him some more honey.

Since then Tough Ted has tried really hard not to moan. But whenever he does, he thinks about the plaster and quickly stops himself before anyone hears! And the rest of the toys do their best to look after him and keep him happy.

The Little Bird

This little bird flaps its wings,
Flaps its wings, flaps its wings,
This little bird flaps its wings,
And flies away in the morning!

Link thumbs and flap fingers

THIS LITTLE BIRD...

Lift hands ...

FLAPS ITS WINGS...

still flapping ...

FLAPS ITS WINGS...

as high as you can

FLIES AWAY...

Two Little Dicky Birds

Stick paper on each index finger

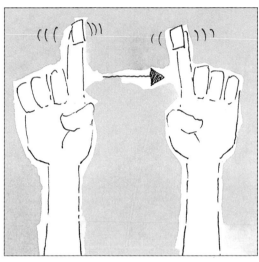

Hold out fingers and shake in turn

Two little dicky birds
Sitting on a wall,

One named Peter,
One named Paul.

Toss each hand behind back

Bring back index fingers in turn

Fly away Peter!
Fly away Paul!

Come back Peter,
Come back Paul.

Sugar and Spice

What are little boys made of?
What are little boys made of?
Frogs and snails
And puppy-dog tails,
That's what little boys are made of.

What are little girls made of?
What are little girls made of?
Sugar and spice
And all things nice,
That's what little girls are made of.

There Was A Little Girl

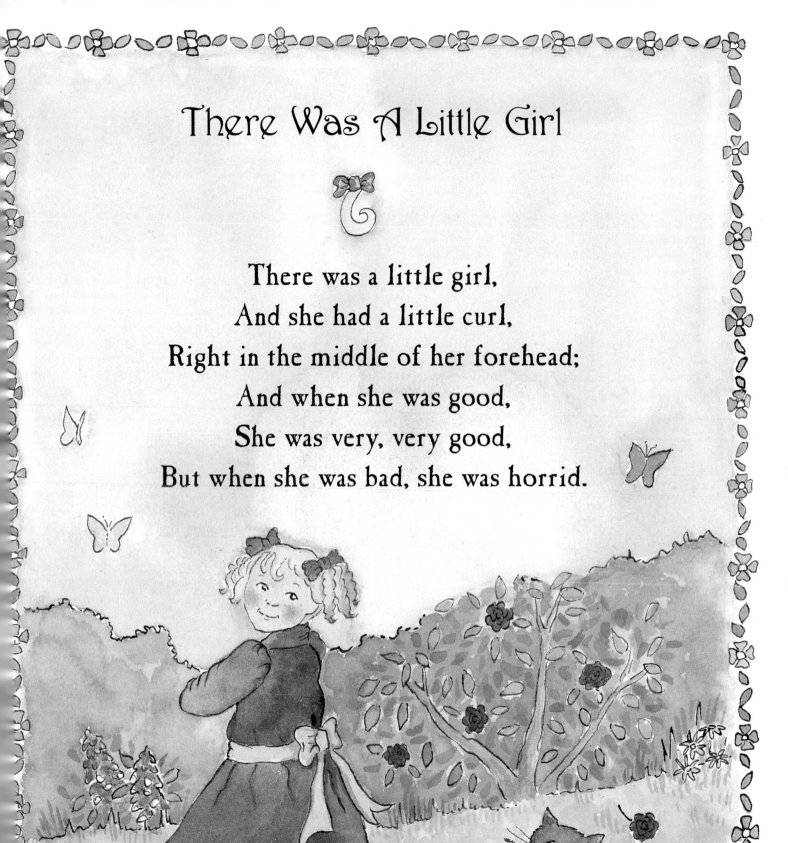

There was a little girl,
And she had a little curl,
Right in the middle of her forehead;
And when she was good,
She was very, very good,
But when she was bad, she was horrid.

Dance To Your Daddy

Dance to your daddy,
My little babby;
Dance to your daddy,
My little lamb.
You shall have a fishy
On a little dishy,
You shall have a fishy
When the boat comes in.

Humpty Dumpty

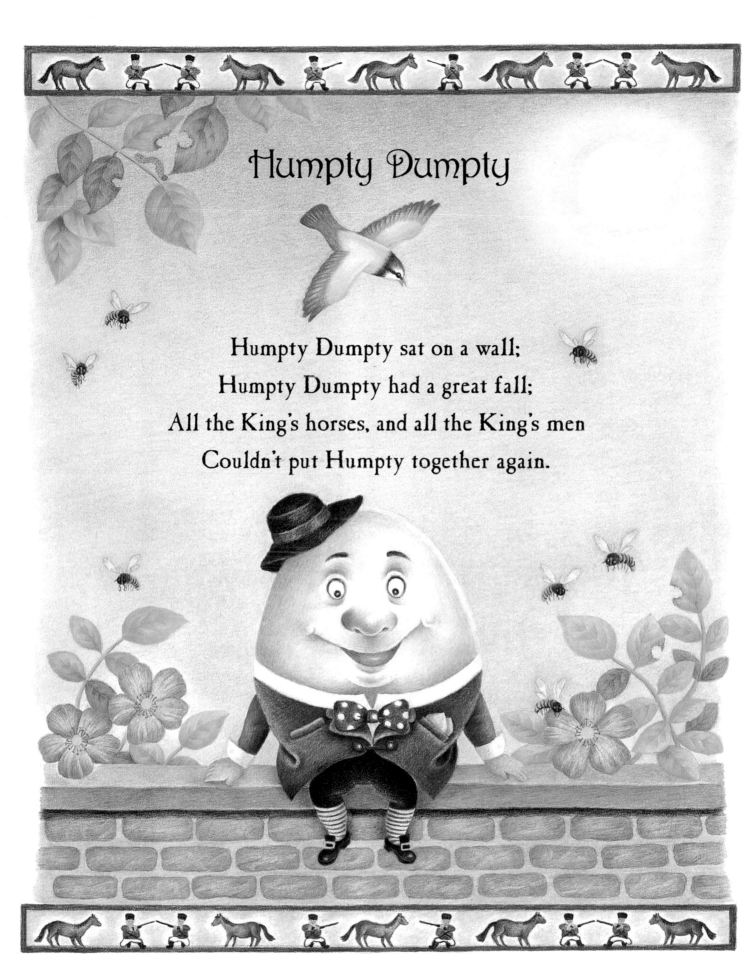

Humpty Dumpty sat on a wall;
Humpty Dumpty had a great fall;
All the King's horses, and all the King's men
Couldn't put Humpty together again.

This is the Way the Ladies Ride

This is the way the ladies ride,
Nimble-nim, nimble-nim.

This is the way the gentlemen ride,
Gallop-a-trot, gallop-a-trot.

This is the way the farmers ride,
Hobbledy-hoy, hobbledy-hoy.

This is the way the butcher boy rides,
Tripperty-trot, tripperty-trot.

Till he falls in a ditch with a flipperty,
Flipperty, flop, flop, FLOP!

Bounce baby on knee, getting faster as rhyme progresses, and 'dropping' baby through knees on last verse

Five Little Ducks

Five little ducks went swimming one day,
Over the hills and far away,
Mother Duck said, "Quack, quack, quack, quack,"
But only four little ducks came back.

Repeat for four, three and two little ducks...

One little duck went swimming one day,
Over the hills and far away,
Mother Duck said, "Quack, quack, quack, quack,"
And all the five little ducks came back.

FIVE LITTLE DUCKS...

OVER THE HILLS...

QUACK, QUACK, QUACK

FOUR LITTLE DUCKS

LEAP FROG

"Whee! Look at me! Look at me!" yelled Springy, the frog, as he went leaping through the air, jumping from one lily pad to the other with a great splash. "I'm the bounciest frog in the whole wide world! Whee!"

"Tut, tut!" quacked Mother Duck. "That young frog is a nuisance. He never looks where he's going, and he doesn't mind who he splashes."

"Quite dreadful," agreed Downy, the swan. "And he makes so much noise. Sometimes it's hard to hear yourself think!"

But Springy wasn't listening. He was far too busy jumping across the lily pads as high as he could.

"Come on!" he called to the little ducklings. "Come over here, we'll have a diving contest!"

The ducklings shook their tails with excitement as they hurried across the pond towards him, then splashed about ducking and diving.

"He's a bad influence on our youngsters," Mother Duck went on. "If only something could be done about him."

"I suppose it's just high spirits," said Downy. "He'll grow out of it."

But Springy didn't grow out of it — he grew worse. He would wake everyone up at the crack of dawn, singing loudly at the top of his croaky voice: "Here comes the day, it's time to play, hip hooray, hip hooray!" And he would leap from place to place, waking up the ducks and swans in their nests, calling down Rabbit's burrow, and shouting into Water Rat's hole in the bank. Of course, Springy just thought that he was being friendly. He didn't realise that everyone was getting fed up with him.

"I'm all for a bit of fun," said Water Rat. "But young Springy always takes things too far."

Then one day, Springy appeared almost bursting with excitement.

"Listen everyone," he called. "There's going to be a jumping competition on the other side of the pond. All the other frogs from miles around are coming. But I'm sure to win, because I'm the bounciest frog in the whole wide world!" And with that he jumped high up in the air, just to prove it was true.

The day of the contest dawned, and everyone gathered at the far side of the pond to watch the competition. Springy had never seen so many frogs in one place before.

"Wait till they see how high I can jump!" he said, leaping up and down in excitement.

But to Springy's amazement, all the frogs could jump high, and far too. They sprang gracefully across the lily pads, cheered on by the crowd.

Springy was going to have to jump higher and further than ever if he wanted to win. At last it was his turn. "Good luck!" cried the ducklings.

Springy took his place on the starting pad, then gathering all his strength, he leapt up high and flew through the air, further and further, past the finish line, and on, until – GULP! He landed right in crafty Pike's waiting open mouth! As usual, Springy had not been looking where he was going!

The naughty pike swallowed Springy in one gulp, then dove down and hid in the middle of the pond. Everyone looked around in dismay — there was nothing they could do. Springy was gone.

Well, there was no doubt about it. Springy had jumped the highest, and the furthest.

"I declare Springy the winner," Warty, the toad, who had organised the contest, said glumly. So everyone went home, feeling sad and empty.

After that, things were much quieter for the other folk that lived around the pond.

But instead of enjoying the peace, they found that they rather missed Springy.

"He was a cheery little frog," said Downy.

"My young ones miss him terribly," said Mother Duck. "I suppose he did keep them busy."

But deep in the pond, Pike was feeling sorry for himself. He thought he'd been very clever catching that frog, but he'd had terrible indigestion ever since. You see, Springy was still busy jumping away inside him! Pike rose up to the top of the water, and gulped at the air. And as he did so, out jumped Springy!

Everyone was delighted to see him, and cheered as they gave him the medal for winning the jumping contest.

"This is wonderful," said Springy. "But I have learned my lesson — from now on I'll look before I leap!" and he hopped away quietly to play with the ducklings.

Where are you Going to, My Pretty Maid?

Where are you going to, my pretty maid?
Where are you going to, my pretty maid?
I'm going a-milking, sir, she said,
Sir, she said, sir, she said,
I'm going a-milking, sir, she said.

May I go with you, my pretty maid?
May I go with you, my pretty maid?
You're kindly welcome, sir, she said,
Sir, she said, sir, she said,
You're kindly welcome, sir, she said.

What is your fortune, my pretty maid?
What is your fortune, my pretty maid?
My face is my fortune, sir, she said,
Sir, she said, sir, she said,
My face is my fortune, sir, she said.

Then I can't marry you, my pretty maid,
Then I can't marry you, my pretty maid,
Nobody asked you, sir, she said,
Sir, she said, sir, she said,
Nobody asked you, sir, she said.

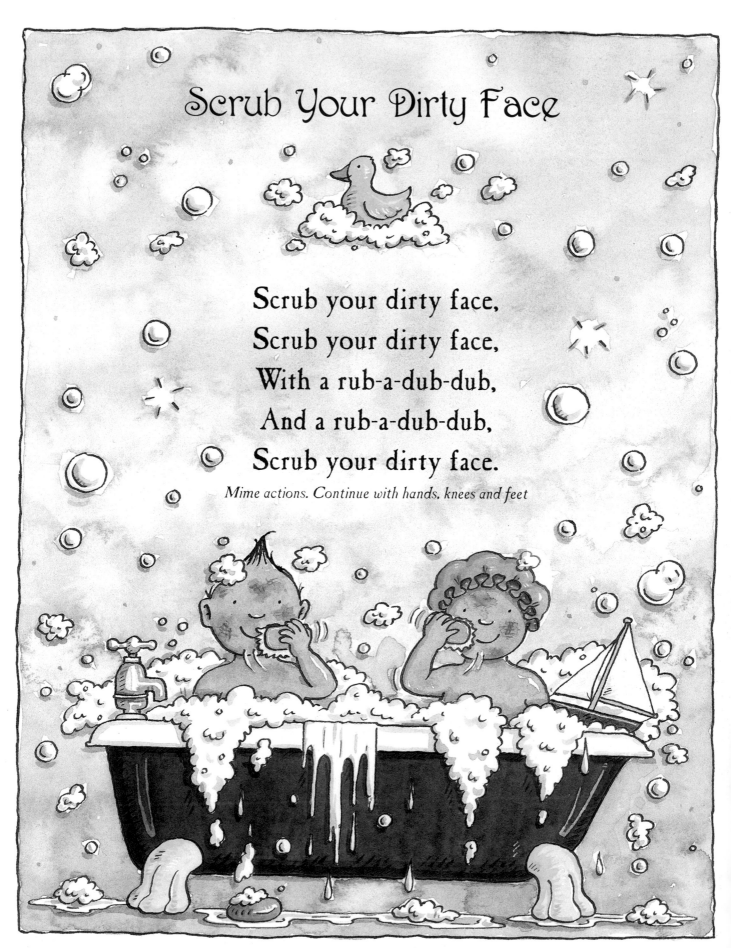

Scrub Your Dirty Face

Scrub your dirty face,
Scrub your dirty face,
With a rub-a-dub-dub,
And a rub-a-dub-dub,
Scrub your dirty face.

Mime actions. Continue with hands, knees and feet

Clap Your Hands

Clap your hands, clap your hands,
Clap them just like me.
Touch your shoulders, touch your shoulders,
Touch them just like me.
Tap your knees, tap your knees,
Tap them just like me.
Shake your head, shake your head,
Shake it just like me.
Clap your hands, clap your hands,
Then let them quiet be.

There Was A Crooked Man

There was a crooked man
And he walked a crooked mile,
He found a crooked sixpence
Against a crooked stile.
He brought a crooked cat
Which caught a crooked mouse
And they all lived together
In a little crooked house.

TEN LITTLE TEDDIES

Ten little teddies, standing in a line,
One of them went fishing, so then there were nine.

Nine little teddies, marching through a gate,
One stopped to tie his shoe, so then there were eight.

Eight little teddies, floating up in heaven,
One fell down and broke his crown,
so then there were seven.

Seven little teddies, doing magic tricks,
One made himself disappear, so then there were six.

Six little teddies, about to take a dive,
One of them was scared of heights, so then there were five.

Five little teddies, running on the shore,
One went surfing in the waves, so then there were four.

Four little teddies, eating cakes for tea,
One of them was feeling sick, so then there were three.

Three little teddies, heading for the zoo,
One of them hopped on a bus, so then there were two.

Two little teddies, playing in the sun,
One of them got sunburnt, so then there was one.

One little teddy, who's had lots of fun,
It's time for him to go to sleep, so now there are none.

The Man in the Moon

The man in the moon
Came down too soon,
And asked his way to Norwich;
He went by the south,
And burnt his mouth
By eating cold plum porridge.

Rock-a-Bye-Baby

Rock-a-bye baby, on the tree top;

When the wind blows, the cradle will rock;

When the bough breaks, the cradle will fall;

Down will come baby, cradle and all.

Five Little Soldiers

Five little soldiers standing in a row,
Three stood straight,

And two stood — so.
Along came the captain,
And what do you think?
They ALL stood straight,
As quick as a wink.

Hold five fingers up

FIVE LITTLE SOLDIERS

Fold down two fingers

AND TWO STOOD - SO

*Pass index finger of
other hand in front*

...WHAT DO YOU THINK

Straighten all fingers

...ALL STOOD STRAIGHT

Here Sits the Lord Mayor

Here sits the Lord Mayor,

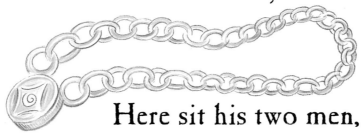

Here sit his two men,

Here sits the cocky,

Here sits the hen,

Here sit the chicks,

And here they run in,

Chin chopper,
chin chopper,
chin chopper,
chin.

329

THE NAUGHTY BEARS

One sunny summer's day, Ben and Fraser's parents told them to pack their things, as they were going to the beach.

"Yippee!" said Ben. "Can we take our teddies?"

"As long as you keep an eye on them," said Daddy. "We don't want to spend all afternoon looking for them if you lose them again!"

Ben and Fraser took their teddies everywhere they went, but they were always losing them, and then there was a great hunt to find them. But the truth was, that when no one was looking, the naughty little teddies would run away in search of excitement and adventure.

Today was no different. The family arrived at the beach and unpacked their things. Daddy sat reading a newspaper and Mommy took out a book. Soon Ben and Fraser were busy building sandcastles. When the naughty teddies saw that no one was looking, they jumped up and ran away giggling, all along the beach.

"Let's go exploring," said Billy, who was the oldest bear. "I can see a cave over there." He pointed to a dark hole in the rocks close to the water.

"It looks a bit dark and scary," said Bella.

"Don't be silly," said Billy. "You're a bear. Bears like dark caves!"

The little bears clambered over the rocks and into the cave. It was very deep, and very dark. Just then, Bella spotted something gleaming on the floor. She picked it up and showed it to Billy.

"Gold!" said Billy, in excitement, taking the little coin from Bella. "This must be a smuggler's cave! Maybe the smugglers are still here. Let's take a look!"

"No!" said Bella. "They could be dangerous. Let's go back." She turned and ran back outside, where she saw to her horror that while they had been exploring the tide had come in, and cut the rocks off from the beach.

"Billy!" she called. "Come quick, we're stranded!"

Meanwhile, Ben and Fraser had finished making sandcastles and found that their teddy bears were missing.

"Oh, no," groaned Daddy. "Not again!"

The family hunted high and low along the beach, but there was no sign of the bears to be found. "Maybe they've been washed out to sea," said Fraser, his voice trembling at the thought.

Back at the cave the naughty teddies could see their owners looking for them. They jumped up and down and waved their paws. "It's no use," said Bella, "they can't see us. We're too small."

"Don't worry," said Billy, trying to sound braver than he felt.

Just then, two men appeared from the other side of the rocks. The teddies froze — these must be the smugglers! They trembled in fear as the men picked them up, clambered over the rocks, and tossed them into a little boat that had been hidden from view. The teddies clung together at the bottom of the boat as the men jumped in and began to row. Where were they taking them?

After a while, the boat stopped and one of the men jumped out. He grabbed the bears and held them in the air high above his head, calling out, "Has anyone lost these bears?"

Everyone on the beach looked up, and Ben and Fraser raced over and grabbed their bears.

"Thank you," said Daddy. "We've been looking everywhere for them."

"We found them up by that cave," said one of the men, pointing over to the cave. "Your kids must have left them there."

"But they've been here building sandcastles all afternoon..." said Daddy, looking puzzled.

No one ever did find out how the naughty teddies got to the cave, or where the little coin in Billy's pocket came from. But from then on Daddy said they had to stay at home. The naughty teddies didn't really mind. They'd had enough adventures for the time being. And it gave them lots of time to play their favorite game – hide and seek!

I Am A Music Man

LEADER: I am a music man,
I come from far away,
And I can play.
ALL: What can you play?
LEADER: I play piano.
ALL: Pia, pia, piano, piano, piano,
Pia, pia, piano, pia, piano.

LEADER: I am a music man,
I come from far away,
And I can play.
ALL: What can you play?
LEADER: I play the big drum.
ALL: Boomdi, boomdi, boomdi boom,
Boomdi boom, boomdi boom,
Boomdi, boomdi, boomdi boom,
Boomdi, boomdi boom.
Pia, pia, piano, piano, piano,
Pia, pia, piano, pia, piano.

LEADER: I am a music man.
I come from far away,
And I can play.

ALL: What can you play?

LEADER: I play the trumpet.

ALL: Tooti, tooti, tooti, toot,
Tooti, toot, tooti, toot,
Tooti, tooti, tooti, toot,
Tooti, tooti, toot.

Boomdi, boomdi, boomdi boom,
Boomdi boom, boomdi boom,
Boomdi, boomdi, boomdi boom,
Boomdi, boomdi boom.

Pia, pia, piano, piano, piano,
Pia, pia, piano, pia, piano.

Pretend to play each instrument in turn

339

With My Hands on Myself

With my hands on myself,
what have we here?
This is my brainbox,
nothing to fear.
Brainbox and wibbly
wobbly woos,
That's what they taught me
when I went to school.

With my hands on myself,
what have we here?
These are my eye-peepers,
nothing to fear.
Eye-peepers, brainbox
and wibbly wobbly woos,
That's what they taught me
when I went to school.

With my hands on myself,
what have we here?
This is my nose-wiper,
nothing to fear.
Nose-wiper, eye-peepers,
brainbox and wibbly
wobbly woos,
That's what they taught me
when I went to school.

With my hands on myself,
what have we here?
This is my chest-protector,
nothing to fear.
Chest-protector, nose-wiper,
eye-peepers, brainbox and
wibbly wobbly woos,
That's what they taught me
when I went to school.

Wibbly woobly woos are the ear lobes, which should be wiggled whenever they are mentioned.
Additional verses could include bread basket (tummy), knee knockers (knees), and shoe stuffers (feet).

Bobby Shaftoe

Bobby Shaftoe's gone to sea,
Silver buckles at his knee,
He'll come back and marry me,
Bonny Bobby Shaftoe.

Little Jack Horner

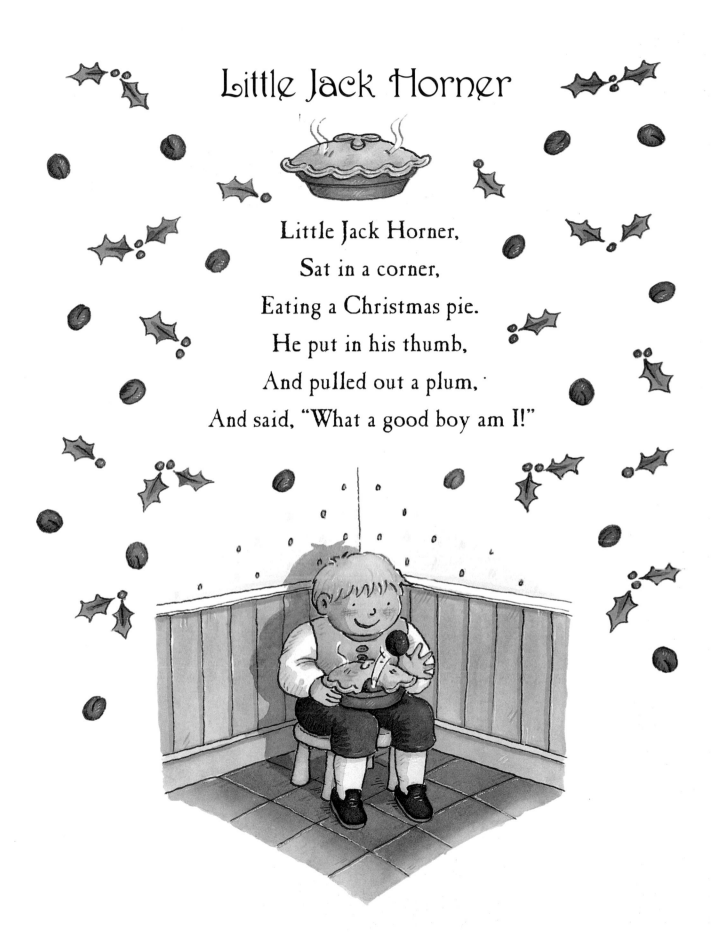

Little Jack Horner,

Sat in a corner,

Eating a Christmas pie.

He put in his thumb,

And pulled out a plum,

And said, "What a good boy am I!"

Jack and Jill

Jack and Jill went up the hill
To fetch a pail of water;
Jack fell down and broke his crown
And Jill came tumbling after.

Up Jack got and home did trot
As fast as he could caper;
He went to bed to mend his head
With vinegar and brown paper.

344

Polly Put The Kettle On

Polly put the kettle on,
Polly put the kettle on,
Polly put the kettle on,
We'll all have tea.

Sukey take it off again,
Sukey take it off again,
Sukey take it off again,
They've all gone away.

Pease Pudding Hot

Pease pudding hot,
Pease pudding cold,
Pease pudding in the pot,
Nine days old.

Some like it hot,
Some like it cold,
Some like it in the pot,
Nine days old.

Sing a Song of Sixpence

Sing a song of sixpence,
A pocket full of rye;
Four-and-twenty blackbirds baked in a pie;
When the pie was opened,
The birds began to sing;
Wasn't that a dainty dish,
To set before a king?

BIRTHDAY BUNNIES

"It's my first birthday tomorrow!" announced Snowy, a little white rabbit, very proudly. "Isn't that exciting?"

"Yes, very exciting!" said Whiskers, her brother. "Because it's my birthday too!"

"And mine!" said Patch.

"And mine!" said Nibble.

"And mine!" said Twitch.

"Do you think mom and dad have got a surprise for us?" asked Snowy.

"I hope so!" said Whiskers.

"Me too!" said Patch.

"Me too!" said Nibble.

"Me too!" said Twitch.

Mrs Rabbit was listening outside the door, as her children were getting ready for bed. She heard the little bunnies chattering excitedly about their birthdays the next day.

Whatever could she do to make it a special day for them? She sat and thought very hard, and later that evening, when Mr Rabbit came home, she said: "It is the childrens' first birthday tomorrow, and I'm planning a surprise for them. I want to make them a carrot cake, but I will need some carrots. Could you go and dig some nice fresh ones up from your vegetable garden?"

"Certainly, dear," said Mr Rabbit, and off he went back outside.

Mr Rabbit was proud of the carrots he grew. They were very fine carrots, crunchy and sweet and delicious. Every year he entered them in the Country Show, and they nearly always won first prize. So you can imagine his dismay when he arrived at his vegetable patch to find that every single carrot had been dug up and stolen!

He marched back inside. "Someone has stolen my carrots!" he announced to his wife, crossly. "And I am going to find out just who it is!"

And although it was getting late, he went back outside, and set off to find the naughty person.

First of all he stopped at Hungry Hare's house, and knocked at the door.

"Someone has stolen my carrots!" Mr Rabbit said. "Do you know who?"

"Oh, yes," said Hungry Hare. "But it wasn't me." And although Mr Rabbit pressed him, Hungry Hare would say no more.

Next Mr Rabbit went to Sly Fox's house.

"Someone has stolen my carrots!" he said. "Do you know who?"

"Oh, yes," said Sly Fox. "But it wasn't me." And although Mr Rabbit begged and pleaded with him, Sly Fox would say no more.

So Mr Rabbit marched to Bill Badger's house, and asked if he knew who had taken the carrots.

"Why, yes, in fact I do," said Bill Badger. "But it wasn't me."

And just like the others, he would say no more. It was the same wherever Mr Rabbit went, and although he got very cross, and stamped his foot, no one would tell him who had stolen his carrots!

"You'll find out soon enough," said Red Squirrel.

So Mr Rabbit went home feeling very puzzled.

"It seems that everyone knows who it was, but no one will tell me!" said Mr Rabbit to his wife.

"Not everyone, dear," she said. "I don't know who it was either. All I know is that it's our childrens' first birthday tomorrow, and we have no surprise for them." And feeling very miserable and confused, they went to bed, determined to get to the bottom of the mystery in the morning.

Next day the little bunnies came running into the kitchen, where their parents were having breakfast.

"Happy birthday, everyone!" called Snowy.

"Happy birthday!" cried the other little bunnies.

"Now, it's not much, but I wanted to give each of you a surprise!" Snowy went on. "By the way, I hope you don't mind, Dad." And with that Snowy pulled out a box of juicy carrots, each tied with a bow, and handed one to each of her brothers and sisters.

"Snap!" cried Whiskers, "I had just the same idea!" and he pulled out another box of carrots.

"Me too!" said Patch.

"Me too!" said Nibble.

"Me too!" said Twitch.

Soon there was a great pile of juicy carrots heaped on the kitchen table.

"So that's what happened to my carrots!" cried Mr Rabbit, in amazement. "I thought they had been stolen! And when he told the little bunnies the story they laughed till their sides ached. Then Mrs Rabbit put on her apron and shooed them outside.

"Just leave the carrots with me," she said.
"I have a birthday surprise of my own in store!"

And so the mystery was solved. It turned out
that Hungry Hare had seen the little bunnies
creep out one by one, and each dig up a few
carrots when they thought no one was looking.
He knew it was their birthdays and he guessed
what they were doing. He had told the other forest
folk, and everyone thought it was a great joke.

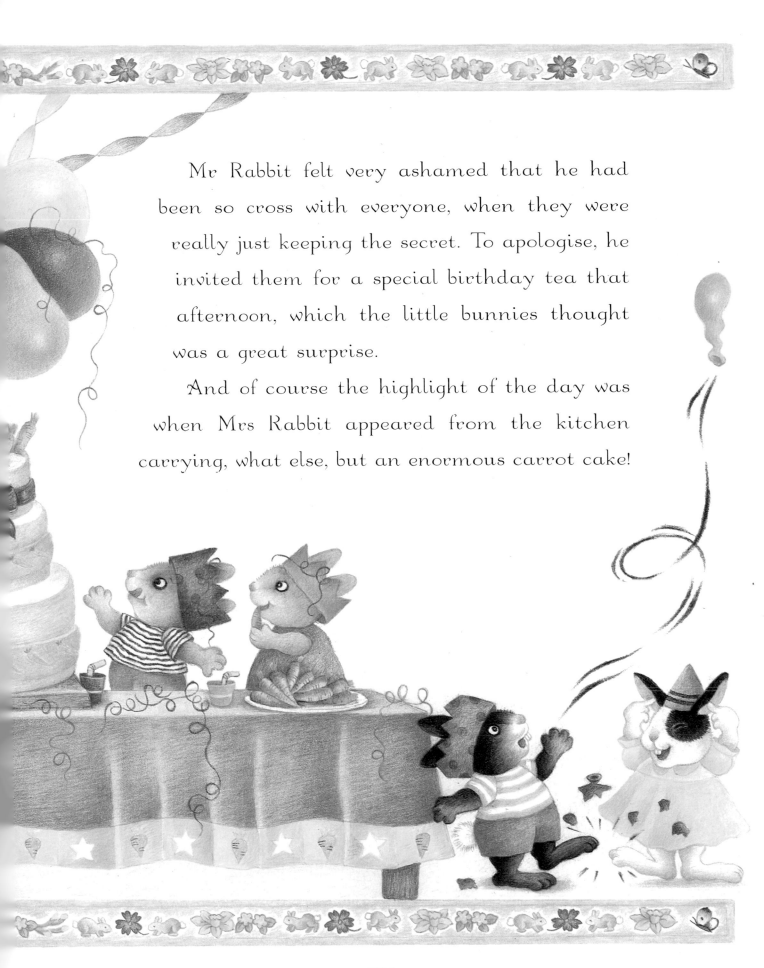

Mr Rabbit felt very ashamed that he had been so cross with everyone, when they were really just keeping the secret. To apologise, he invited them for a special birthday tea that afternoon, which the little bunnies thought was a great surprise.

And of course the highlight of the day was when Mrs Rabbit appeared from the kitchen carrying, what else, but an enormous carrot cake!

The North Wind

The north wind doth blow,
And we shall have snow,
And what will poor
robin do then?
Poor thing.

He'll sit in a barn,
And keep himself warm,
And hide his head
under his wing,
Poor thing.

Whether the Weather

Whether the weather be fine,
Or whether the weather be not,
Whether the weather be cold,
Or whether the weather be hot,
We'll weather the weather
Whatever the weather,
Whether we like it or not!

One, Two, Three, Four, Five

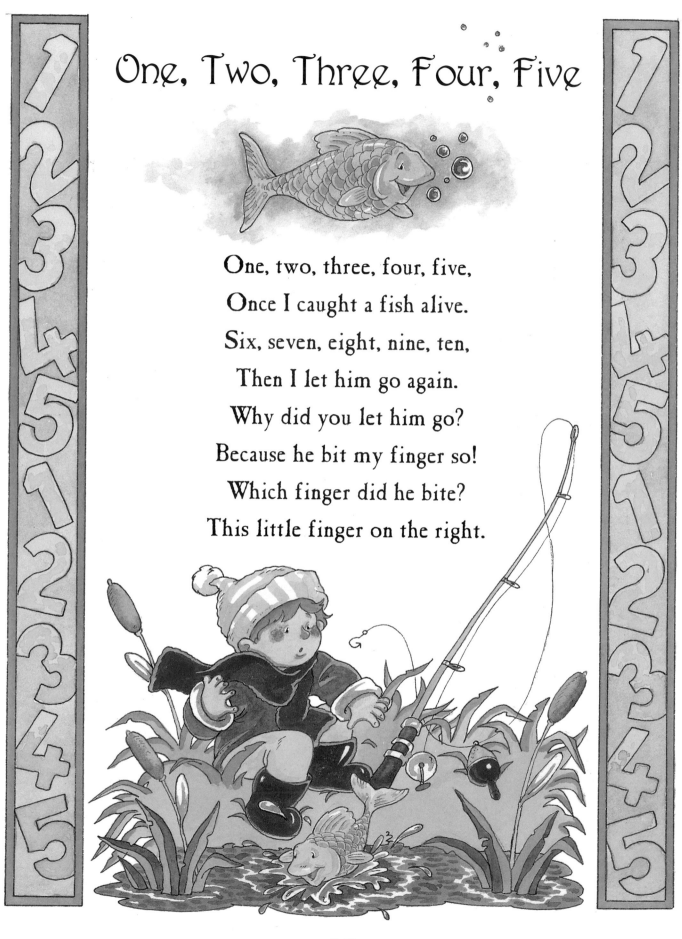

One, two, three, four, five,

Once I caught a fish alive.

Six, seven, eight, nine, ten,

Then I let him go again.

Why did you let him go?

Because he bit my finger so!

Which finger did he bite?

This little finger on the right.

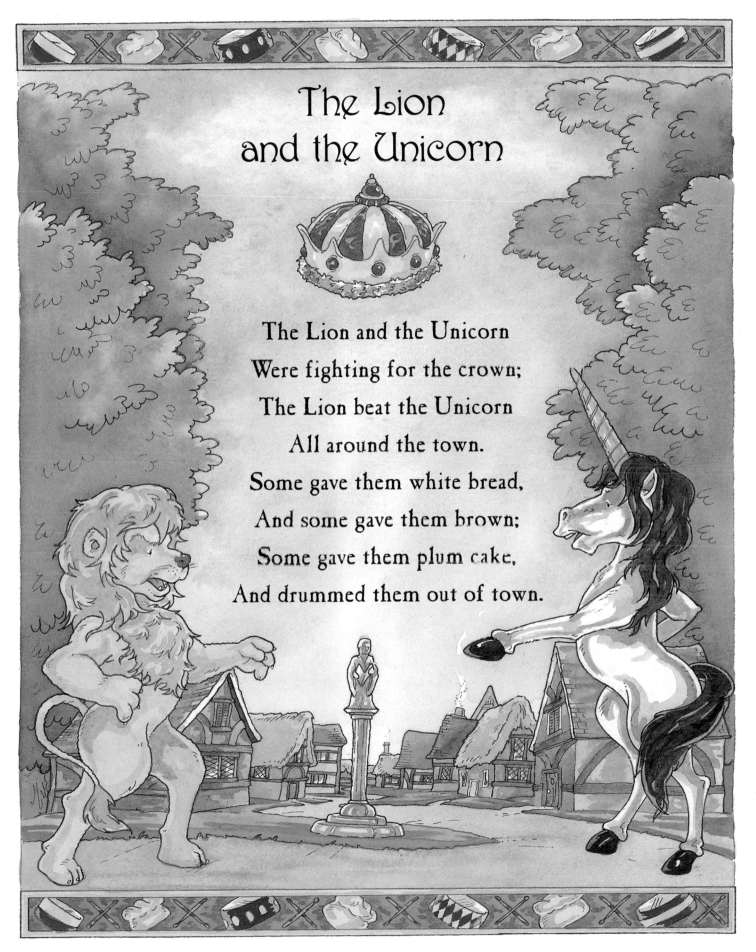

The Lion
and the Unicorn

The Lion and the Unicorn

Were fighting for the crown;

The Lion beat the Unicorn

All around the town.

Some gave them white bread,

And some gave them brown;

Some gave them plum cake,

And drummed them out of town.

Hey De Ho

Hey de, hey de ho,
The great big elephant
Is so slow.
Hey de, hey de ho,
The elephant is so slow.

He swings his tail
From side to side,
As he takes the children
For a ride.

Hey de, hey de ho,
The elephant is so slow.

LITTLE SHEEP

Little Sheep couldn't sleep,
Not a wink, not a peep!
Tossing, turning, all night through,
What was poor Little Sheep to do?

Owl came by, old and wise,
Said, "Silly sheep, use your eyes –
You're lying in a field of sheep,
Try counting them to help you sleep!"

"Seven, four, thirteen, ten –
That's not right, I'll start again..."
Till daylight came, awake he lay
And vowed he'd learn to count next day!

GIRAFFE'S SONG

It's wonderful having a long neck,
That reaches right up to the sky,
You can nibble the leaves on the treetops,
And smile at the birds flying by.

It's wonderful having a long neck,
You can see for miles around,
You always know just where
your friends are,
And where the best food can be found.

It's wonderful having a long neck,
Although, I'm not meaning to gloat.
For there's one time that I really curse it,
And that's when I get a sore throat!

Little Boy Blue

Little Boy Blue, come blow your horn

The sheep's in the meadow, the cow's in the corn.

Where is the boy who looks after the sheep?

He's under the haystack fast asleep.

Will you wake him? No, not I!

For if I do, he's sure to cry.

Yankee Doodle

Yankee Doodle came to town,

Riding on a pony,

He stuck a feather in his cap

And called it macaroni.

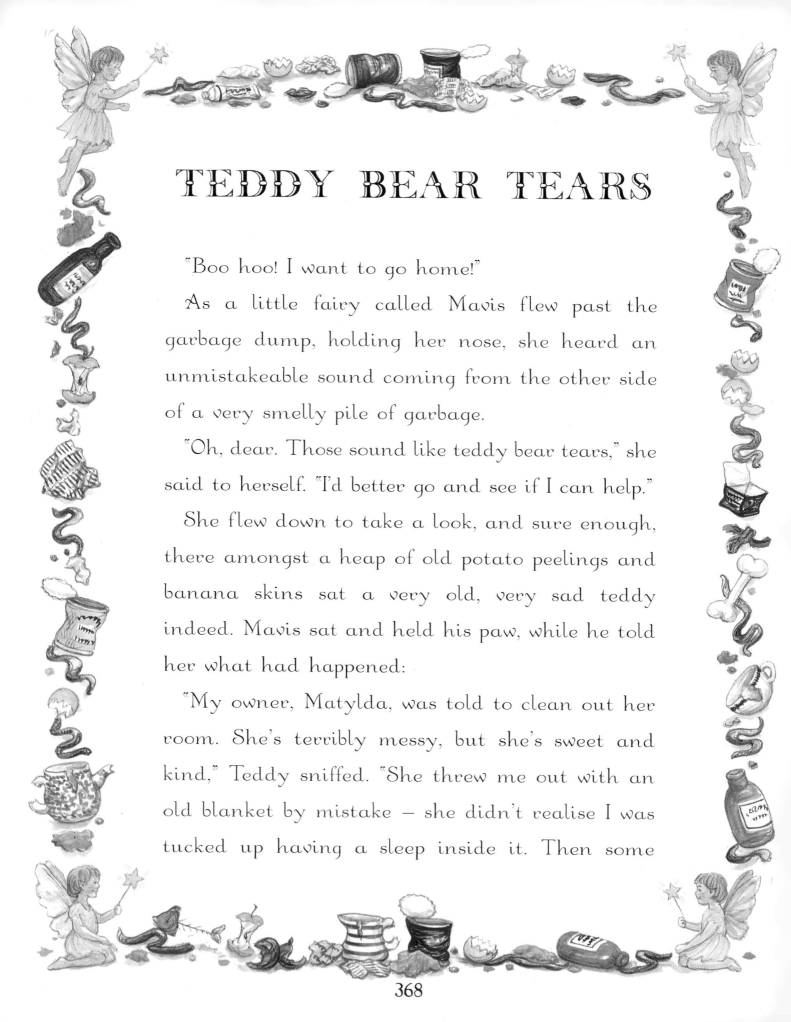

TEDDY BEAR TEARS

"Boo hoo! I want to go home!"

As a little fairy called Mavis flew past the garbage dump, holding her nose, she heard an unmistakeable sound coming from the other side of a very smelly pile of garbage.

"Oh, dear. Those sound like teddy bear tears," she said to herself. "I'd better go and see if I can help."

She flew down to take a look, and sure enough, there amongst a heap of old potato peelings and banana skins sat a very old, very sad teddy indeed. Mavis sat and held his paw, while he told her what had happened:

"My owner, Matylda, was told to clean out her room. She's terribly messy, but she's sweet and kind," Teddy sniffed. "She threw me out with an old blanket by mistake — she didn't realise I was tucked up having a sleep inside it. Then some

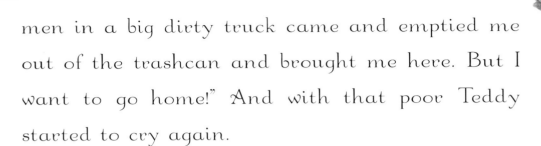

men in a big dirty truck came and emptied me out of the trashcan and brought me here. But I want to go home!" And with that poor Teddy started to cry again.

"There, there," said Mavis. "I'll help to get you home. But first I'll need two teddy bear tears." She unscrewed the lid of a little jar, and scooped two big salty tears into it from Teddy's cheeks.

"What do you need those for?" asked Teddy, feeling rather bewildered.

"Just a little fairy magic!" said Mavis. "Now wait here, and I promise I'll be back soon." And with a wave of her wand she disappeared.

Teddy pulled the blanket around him, and sat trying to be brave, and not to cry. He stayed like that all night, feeling cold and alone and frightened. How he wished he was back in his warm cozy home.

Meanwhile Mavis was very busy. She flew back and forth around the neighborhood, until she heard the sound of sobbing coming from an open window. She flew down onto the window sill and peered inside. A little girl was lying on the bed, with her mommy sitting beside her.

"I want my teddy!" she cried.

"Well if you weren't so messy Matylda, you wouldn't lose things," said Mommy gently.

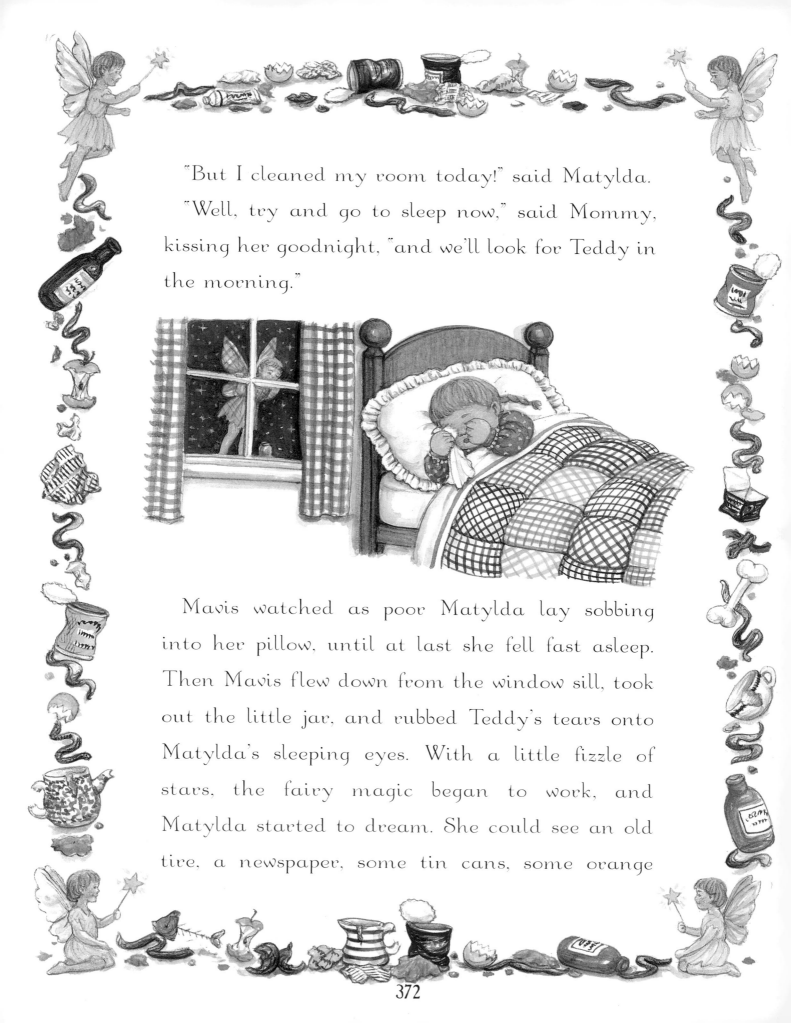

"But I cleaned my room today!" said Matylda.

"Well, try and go to sleep now," said Mommy, kissing her goodnight, "and we'll look for Teddy in the morning."

Mavis watched as poor Matylda lay sobbing into her pillow, until at last she fell fast asleep. Then Mavis flew down from the window sill, took out the little jar, and rubbed Teddy's tears onto Matylda's sleeping eyes. With a little fizzle of stars, the fairy magic began to work, and Matylda started to dream. She could see an old tire, a newspaper, some tin cans, some orange peel, a blanket... wait a minute, it was her blanket, and there, wrapped inside it was her teddy, with a big tear running down his cheek! Teddy was at the garbage dump!

The next morning, Matylda woke with a start, and remembered her dream at once. She ran downstairs to the kitchen, where Mommy was making breakfast, and told her all about it.

"We have to go to the garbage dump! We have to save Teddy!" said Matylda.

Mummy tried to explain that it was just a dream, but Matylda wouldn't listen, so in the end they set off to take a look.

They arrived just as a big machine was scooping up the rubbish and heading for the crusher. And there, on top of the scoop, clinging to the edge, was Teddy!

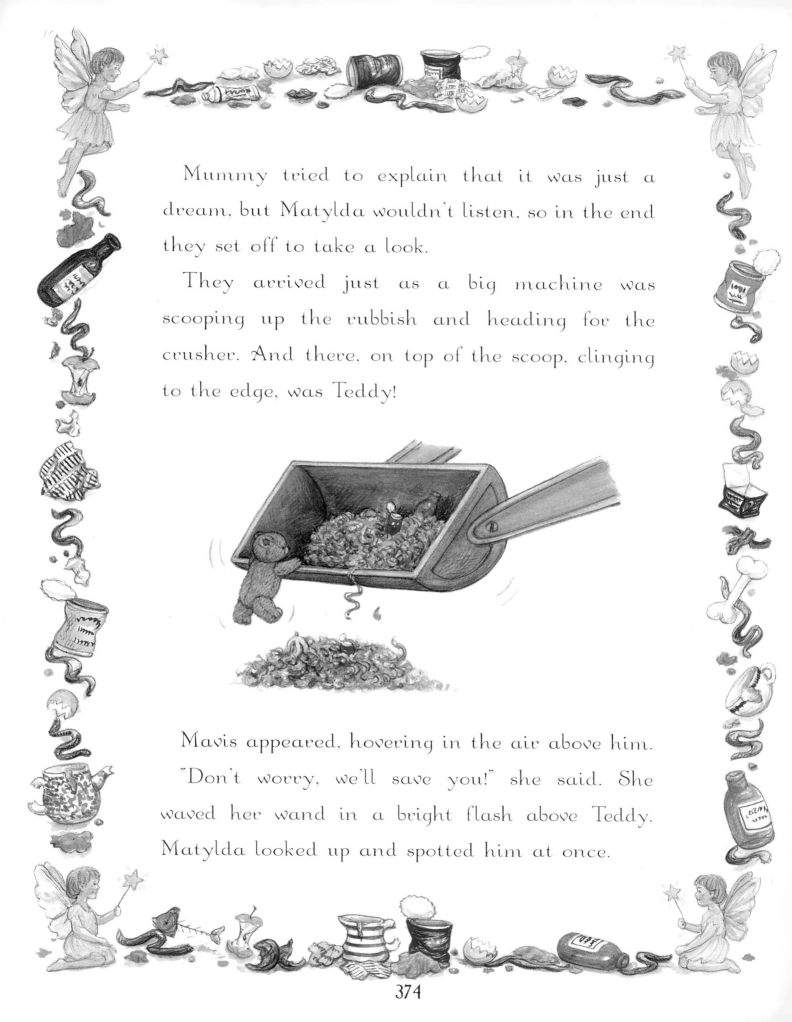

Mavis appeared, hovering in the air above him. "Don't worry, we'll save you!" she said. She waved her wand in a bright flash above Teddy. Matylda looked up and spotted him at once.

"There he is!" she cried, pointing frantically at Teddy. "He's going to be squashed! Mummy, do something, quick!" Mummy ran up to the man driving the machine, waving her arms in the air.

He stopped his machine just in time.

Soon Teddy and Matylda were reunited, and there were more tears, although this time they were happy ones. And from then on, Matylda's room was the tidiest room you have ever seen.

Mary, Mary, Quite Contrary

Mary, Mary, quite contrary,
How does your garden grow?
With silver bells and cockle shells
And pretty maids all in a row.

A Tisket, A Tasket

A tisket, a tasket,
A green and yellow basket.
I wrote a letter to my love,
And on the way I dropped it.

I dropped it, I dropped it,
And on the way I dropped it.
A little girl picked it up
And put it in her pocket.

Higgledy-Piggledy

Higgledy-Piggledy,
My black hen,
She lays eggs for gentlemen;
Sometimes nine,
And sometimes ten,
Higgledy-Piggledy, my black hen!

Oats and Beans

Oats and beans and barley grow,
Oats and beans and barley grow,
Do you or I or anyone know,
How oats and beans and barley grow?

First the farmer sows his seeds,
Then he stands and takes his ease,
Stamps his feet and claps his hands,
Turns around to view the land.

Ding Dong Bell

Ding, dong, bell,

Pussy's in the well!

Who put her in?

Little Tommy Green.

Who pulled her out?

Little Johnny Stout.

What a naughty boy was that

To try to drown poor pussy cat,

Who never did any harm,

But killed the mice in his father's barn.

Dance, Thumbkin, Dance

Make thumbs dance

Dance, dance, thumbkin, dance.
Dance ye merrymen everyone.
Thumbkin he can dance alone,
He can dance alone.

Dance, dance, foreman, dance.
Dance ye merrymen everyone.
Foreman he can dance alone,
He can dance alone.

Dance, dance, longman, dance.
Dance ye merrymen everyone.
Longman he can dance alone,
He can dance alone.

Dance, dance, ringman, dance.
Dance ye merrymen everyone.
Ringman he can dance alone,
He can dance alone.

Dance, dance, babyman, dance.
Dance ye merrymen everyone.
Babyman he can dance alone,
He can dance alone.

THE END

Illustrations by:
Georgie Birkett, Stephanie Boey, Mario Capaldi, Dorothy Clark,
Kate Davies, Maggie Downer, Frank Endersby, Serena Feneziani,
Andrew Geeson, Piers Harper, Elaine Keary, Angela Kincaid, Jane Molineaux,
Claire Mumford, Rikki O'Neill, Pauline Siewart, Jessica Stockham, Linda Worrell.